The Necromancer

Douglas Clegg

**THIS SPECIAL SIGNED EDITION
IS LIMITED TO 1,500 COPIES.**

The Necromancer

The Necromancer

Being the Diary of Justin Gravesend On the Year of his Rebirth, and his FORCED INITIATION into the Chymera Magick, including his EARLY visionaries.

Douglas Clegg

CEMETERY DANCE PUBLICATIONS

Baltimore
❖ 2003 ❖

Signed Hardcover Edition   ISBN 1-58767-071-2

The Necromancer Copyright © 2003
by Douglas Clegg

Artwork Copyright © 2003 by Caniglia

This book is a work of fiction. Names, characters, places, and incidents are either a product of the author's imagination or are used fictitiously. Any resemblance to actual events or locals or persons, living or dead, is entirely coincidental.

All Rights Reserved.

Manufactured in the United States of America.

FIRST EDITION

Cemetery Dance Publications
132-B Industry Lane
Unit 7
Forest Hill, MD 21050
Email: info@cemeterydance.com

www.cemeterydance.com

For Melisse, a story of debauchery and darkness for you, and a borrowed name. To be shared with M.J. Rose.

Somnia, terrores magicos, miracula, fagas, nocturnos lemures, portentaques…
—*Horace*

All places shall be hell that is not heaven.
—*Christopher Marlowe, Dr. Faustus*

Brief Note from Douglas Clegg

The early tales of Harrow are drawn from diaries and fragments of diaries, for the most part. This diary, of Justin Gravesend's early life, is one of several he kept during his lifetime. Additionally, he encouraged the keeping of diaries by his wife and mistresses when he was an older man, no doubt to enhance whatever fame or delusions of grandeur he had.

What is perhaps most remarkable, to me, was the discovery of poem fragments in this diary. I include with this document an introduction by an esteemed academician whose primary studies have been in the history of the occult and classical mythology. Additionally, I have placed Gravesend's so-called "Visionaries" in the order in which he had set them, on separate sheets of parchment, within the diary itself, as if place markers of some sort.

To read more of Harrow, I refer you to my novels, *Mischief, The Infinite,* and *Nightmare House.*

Introduction from a Student of the Necromancer's Diary

As someone who researches the arcane and the unusual artifact of mystical significance, I chanced upon this diary purely by accident while researching a series of grisly murders that occurred in London in the mid-1800s. These were lesser-known killings than the more famous Whitechapel murders attributed to one Jack the Ripper decades later. My hunch as to why these murders did not become better known is that the authorities did not know what to make of them, given the condition of the bodies, and because there was the hint of scandal of an upper class sort around them (for four of the victims were eventually identified), that it was kept quiet in all but the highest circles. There is also the peculiar nature of their discovery: the six victims included two young men of good family, two women, also of good family. They had been entirely eviscerated, their facial features obliterated so that it was difficult if not impossible in some cases to identify them, and on their bodies, occult symbols and monstrous creatures had been tattooed, to the extent that not an inch was left that was not somehow painted over with the tattoo. In going over papers at Scotland Yard, in their historic records library, I learned of the existence of this diary, or rather fragment of a diary, and, through a series of collectors, managed to purchase a photocopy of it, which I'm reprinting here. Some of the pages were illegible or drawn over with symbols and a language that I could not precisely translate, if it was anything more than nonsense.

The nature of a diary is not toward narrative. It is an accounting of events, generally in order. Certain unnessecary sections have been eliminated, including Gravesend's obsessive bookkeeping, house accounting, as well as his sketches and diagrams of both the human body and of fantastical machines that are his ideas, apparently, of how to either torture a human being, or how to drill into the earth. The stuff of science fiction novels or pornography. This diary in your hands is slightly different, for there is something of a narrative, to it, although this utterly falls apart in its latter half. It is not about order, but about disorder, and this seemed to speak to the state of mind of its author. If we are to believe there is some truth to Gravesend's grand conspiracy, of Watchers who follow his moves and direct him to his fateful destination, we would give in to the madness that was Gravesend himself. As you perhaps have read from other books written about the man, he was "the most evil man in existence," or at least that is what the newspapers called him, when he held his famous "Summoning Demons" parties of the late 1800s at his magnificent estate called Harrow. We must understand a little of Gravesend in his later life to put this account of his youth into context.

While Gravesend died in the mid-1920s, outliving his own son, he was not a well-known personage of his time, except among occult circles, and I suspect he enjoyed keeping it that way. In younger years, he had some fame, primarily from claiming that he was bringing in what he called the Age of Baphomet into the world through spiritual endeavors and gatherings that read like a Who's Who of the occult world. (This information can easily be found in the other books related to Gravesend, including the famous memoir, *The Oracle,* by the mysterious Isis Claviger, a clairvoyant of the early 20th century who claimed to be the reincarnation of one of Gravesend's first human sacrifices, but who also claimed she was a reincarnation of Astarte, a priestess of the ancient world, who was the mythic founder of the Chymera Magick and of the flower called herein "Lotos.")

What is remarkable is that at such a young age, he was willing to keep record of these grisly and immoral goings-on of his early life. That he was willing to write down the secrets of this legendary group, the Chymera Magick, and at least a fragment of its initiation rituals which primarily have to do with sex and murder.

A note on the Chymera Magick: this was an order of occultists whose aim is unknown, but which claimed to have originated in Egyptian and Greek Mystery religions, combined with a shoddy alchemy and sense of Black Magic, in the 19th century mystical way of thinking of it. Stealing slightly from the Quabbalah and the Eastern traditions, as well as from the medieval sense of witchcraft and divination, the Chymera Magick seemed to disband in 1914, although I believe it merely went further underground. The infamous book of the Chymerians (as they called themselves) has never been recovered, although Gravesend refers to it within this mishmash of a diary that seems half-brag of his sexual exploits and half-delight in the horror of his devilry. *The Grimoire Chymera*, as it is called, is most likely a fabrication.

The stories surrounding the *Grimoire Chymera* include: the ability to change shape within a range of creatures: to a wolf, to a raven, to serpent. The ability to change between man and woman and back again. The language, or as the Chymerians had it, "The Words," of something called The Veil of the Profane, a place reached with something akin to the opium pipe with the extract of a plant they simply called "Lotos." While we don't know what plant this is, there is a good chance that Gravesend and his fellow Chymerians were simply "chasing the dragon," in opium dens which were popular during much of his life. Additionally, there was the usual—and nearly hackneyed—idea of changing base metals to gold, of acquiring wealth through the mental and magnetic enslavement of others of lesser will, and of maps of the ancient, buried world wherein occult treasures could be found. The key to all mystical texts also supposedly could be found in the *Grimoire Chymera:* the code of the Bible, the genuine translation of the sayings of Jesus, the spells within the epic of Gilgamesh, among other items lesser known today. The *Grimoire* also contained the exact formula for gravity defiance, that individual human flight could be possible

The Necromancer

with the application of a salve on the skin and a long bout of meditation. Purportedly, there was the way to become invisible, briefly, to murder someone by simply kissing them on the neck, and to read the minds of the weakest among humankind in order to have dominion over them. There was also a section in this book that went into the thousand names of the gods, and why mankind had lost the ability to speak directly to them.

It is a grand mythos that the Chymera Magick introduced through their circle, and it is my guess that they duped many of their members into believing that they were anything more than a fraternity of murder, greed, and sexual licentiousness.

More specifically, the life of Justin Gravesend began and ended in his 21st year when he left school and went to London, where he first met the man who would be his Mage, his Guide, his Master through his initiation into the Chymera Magick. He refers to this man as The Necromancer, giving him no Christian name whatsoever, and by this title we know him, and have no idea what further exploits this Necromancer may have had. The Necromancer is obviously a bisexual deviant, someone who finds greatest gratification in perversion, and who is very likely, by the standards of his day, a sadist in the tradition of the writings of the Marquis de Sade (of which, no doubt, Justin and his contemporaries knew well.) While the Necromancer has his share of young women, in a Casanova-like style, he seems peculiarly attracted to men, using them for what he called "Sex Magick," which seems to be none other than sexual deviancy disguised as a transformative experience.

Certainly, young Justin Gravesend came under his tutelage, and experienced what he considered orgiastic visions. But we must remember that these are the words of a young man, experimenting with narcotics and sex and what he calls "the disordering of the senses," through violence. "Awaking the sleeping beast," is his other phrase, and seems to be a philosophy of the Chymerians, in general.

It will be of note that this diary merely ends. It does not reach a satisfactory conclusion, and it is perhaps the beginning of a second diary that Gravesend might've kept. We know, of his life after his 21st year, that he became a captain of industry, a robber baron of sorts, and then retired early, to build his greatest creation, the house known as Harrow, up the Hudson River of New York. Despite amassing great wealth and building an estate of considerable proportions, after his time with the Necromancer, Gravesend seemed to enter a quiet period of his life. In his 30s, he married, raised a family, and although other legends have been connected to the man and his home, he settled down in much the same way that young people everywhere settle down to a life of comparable normalcy. By the age of 46 he was entirely retired, living as landed gentry at Harrow. The house went to his grandson, and then to someone outside the family, named Alfred Barrow, who eventually turned it into, and sold it off as, a school. When the school shut down, it went through at least two ownerships, dogged as any architectural madness might be, by legends of crime and murder and haunting. (I have visited the grounds of Harrow, in late 2002, although it is now completely closed off from the road, with razor wire and ugly

The Necromancer

chainlink fences, a blight on the natural beauty of the area surrounding it, like a pre-Berlin Wall Checkpoint Charlie.)

I have tried to track down the real person who is behind the title, Necromancer, but so far, my pursuit has been unsuccessful.

One thing the sharp reader will notice is that, despite his writing in the 1800s, Gravesend seems to have a 20th century perspective on his adventures. This has led more than one scholar (see Emil Marquand's thesis, presented to the Prague International Occult Congress, 2000, on "The Occult Elite in America and England: 1850—1900") to postulate that Gravesend himself did not write the diary at the time he experienced it, but perhaps dictated it to a secretary of some sort when he was an older man. While this seemingly moot point can be ignored, it is a possibility of which to be aware while reading of these miscreant and diabolical (in the classical sense) adventures.

Editor's Note: Owing to Gravesend's lack of precise dates for his diary entries, we have taken it upon ourselves to divide the Diary into chapters, for easier divisions of events and occurrences. The so-called "Visionaries," as Gravesend called his drug-induced dreams, are set off as their own subsections. These were notes, nearly poems, which should not be taken at face value, as I believe they were Gravesend's poetic mysticism, more savage than Blake's, perhaps, but similar in that they are to be taken as fantasies—often sexual—of a disturbed and possibly addicted mind. We did not set them down in any particular order. Although they are numbered 1, 2, 3, etc., they were gathered in piles, torn from other notebooks, included here as an illumination of the state of mind of Justin Gravesend in his youth.

James Wandigaux, Ph.D., Professor Emeritus, The College of Arts and Sciences, Rutherford University, Surrey, New York

PART ONE

A ddarlenno, ysteried
(translated from the Welsh: Let him who reads, reflect.)

The magician must stand in the posture of supplication, lifting the sacrifice from the field of time into the great sea beyond the Veil, ensuring that the six great pleasures are enacted with regard to the energy points, and the openings are sealed with flesh. Thereby shall he ask nothing of the devourers that he would not ask of himself, and there shall he offer the meat with praise and thanksgiving, for the meat is the life of the devourers, and without meat, there is no sacrifice, and without sacrifice, there is no transformation...
From the Grimoire Chymera

Behold, the architecture of your life
    Alive, In these bones
    Passing into my hands
    How you speak to me of Tyre and Sodom!
  O, sound the ram's horn of Jericho's passing!
Make the heavens shake, and below, the Devils cry!
Each man must die, each city fall
To kiss our Mother Death, laughing, in her pall.

— Justin Gravesend, from *Mother Death Speaks*

Visionary 1

She slams my head back against the wall, and holds her hand against my chest, pushing down upon the area above my heart, tearing at the slender hairs around my nipple, her spit landing on my eye as I slap her across her face, and reach for her hair, pulling it back as hard as I can; I manage to roll on top of her and cover her biting mouth with my gloved hand, and when I let go, she cries out, "Yes, please, yes, yes, sweet, sweet," and then I feel the building of the orgiastic light as waves of undiluted pleasure, set free from conscience, rise within me, within me and my willing partner; she is going there with me, she is giving herself to our destination, and I press myself into her opening flower, holding myself there for the count of one, two, three, four, five, and then the Veil opens before my eyes, and for the first time I see the creature with the three mouths and the fingers like talons, and in its eyes, a feral kindness, like the wolf-cub found in the woods, and I watch, as if floating in the air before it, as it spreads its seven translucent wings and tears greedily into the offered sacrifice.

It wants the throat.

The sacrifice turns her head slightly, to offer.

Her throat is a delight; it is a torment; it is meat.

It is the first milk from a mother, the first taste of life.

Chapter One
My First Birth and Family

1

I was told that the night I was born, my mother saw a terrible face at the window of the midwife's house, of a man who seemed the very Devil.

Given that I have spent most of my life in the Devil's shadow, I believe my mother saw the truth.

2

I was born a monster, and I grew from a monstrous life, and if you read of this, you will understand. I had no choice in my monstrosity.

Fate takes us by the hand and leads us where we are meant to go, and, in turn, we bite her for the pleasure of it. I am a murderer and a scoundrel, but once, I was a child, just as you once have been. Once I sought the goodness of all creation.

Once, I was a common urchin in a tidal pool, surrounded by eagerly devouring eels.

It is all a charade! This life! How we see it! How I saw my own! My life was never my own, but was drawn up as if by a great draughtsman, this Necromancer who had found the relics and used them to enslave me and bring me into the Veil!

I should have burned my books and instead turned to the quiet rustic life to which I had been born, and died with coal-dust in my throat and seven babies 'round the room, and a wife at the hearth! Instead, I allowed the curse that had been laid upon me at the hour of my birth to grow and fester. I followed my will, my flesh, and those who guided me, to this most wondrous and terrible place! Read this and know!

I have seen the other side of existence and it has torn away all conscience from me, and yet, I love the horror more than I love life itself and would not turn back if given the choice.

3

Pleasure and its humours in the human body are what allow us to experience the mystical world. My first pleasure was my mother's nipple and my last, in my twenty-first year, was found at the breast of the Whore of Babylon, that visionary salve, that nectar of the necropolis, the supreme Lotos of the Visionary.

Why me? We each cry, alone, to the universe, to the mute gods or God. Why this fate? Why my destiny and not the destiny of the comfortable life, free of terror and abominations of the flesh? Why not the hypocritical, cushioned life of the normal man? Why not the world in

The Necromancer

which God is for Sundays and life consists of hours of labor followed by a few hours of entertainment and rest? Why this soul searing?

This I cannot answer satisfactorily. I was chosen before I even knew a choice could be made. My only answer can be that it was destiny itself, carved on my bones and sung within the chambers of my heart.

I had a sponsor to bring me to the attention of that secret society called the Chymera Magick. I could not have avoided my destiny had I desired to do so.

My life is written on my skin, tattooed as surely as if needles had been pressed into me, in the pathways of my blood, and the subcutaneous layers, the prick of life—and of the Occult Arts—dug chigger-like into me, and it is there. We are not mind, although we feel we are. We are body, we are flesh, we are the points of hair and the torn skin, and it is the obliteration of the mind that brings us in contact with the visions and the truth. It is through the destruction of social hypocrisy, of taboo, of restraint, that opens us up, that finds doorways where there have been none, and bores holes into us, opening us to the vibrant hum of the cosmos. In the story of my life, you will read of terrible things, by your standards. You will read of vows broken, of demons raised, of bodies used unnaturally, of deviancy, and unholy ritual, of nuns brought into the orgy pit, and of men used as women, and women used as men. Do not flinch from this, for that is the squint of the weak human mind that we believe we possess.

Use these shocking acts as a way of awakening the creature within its cage.

The one who is the Many. The Lord of the Flies is no Devil. The Lord of Pestilence is no beekeeper of souls.

He is our brother.

Use this to gain wisdom and seek your heaven. I have seen the afterworld, and I will tell you it is more terrible than the worst tortures of this fair land. Do you walk the Earth and believe it unmerciful and unjust? The life beyond this one is ten thousand times more horrible. It is a screaming moment frozen in an eternal chamber of torment. You would do well to seek the disordering of your senses now, to ungird yourselves of your weighty prison of the mind and unleash every desire of your flesh, every forbidden thing you can imagine, let it come to pass. For the end of your life already circles around you. You shall be bitten by its ravening silver teeth, and torn by its pincers. You must embrace it and open yourself to it.

As I did.

4

I came into the world feeling as if something important had been taken from me. And it is this, more than my want of wealth and power and happiness, that has driven me to my current state.

My name is Justin Gravesend, although this was not my name at birth.

Then, I was named Iestyn, a Welsh form of Justin, meaning, of course, "the just." It was an old-fashioned name to have when I was a boy, but it was a relief to avoid the Biblical names that were so popular then. I was born near an ancient colliery and its spoil heaps, in operation since the Middle Ages, which seemed

The Necromancer

fitting since it was its own kind of torture chamber. The coalfields were the dark heart of all our existences, with the wool industry taking second place. The village where I grew up was small then, called Cwthshire, pronounced Coo-shire, and our nearest city, a good forty miles, was called Llangolen, and even that was not much of a city then. I am sorry to say that our little village no longer exists, abandoned when the local mining ended with several explosions that killed many miners and closed off the mine itself.

When I was a child, it was my kingdom.

We lived near three rivers, one wide and broad that ran through the village, tamed as a canal before my birth, called the Range for a reason I never have understood, and two slimmer ones that seemed mere streams to me as a boy. I did not speak Welsh well, owing in part to the fact that my parents both discouraged it. We were not really a Welsh family, although my father's Welshness-by-way-of-Manchester-and-Liverpool existed in much the same way as my mother's slight Irishness: in a few names, a few phrases, and not much else. They had arrived in Cwthshire to find work and life in the colliery and the sheep meadows. My mother was Catholic, from Ireland by way of Scotland by way of Cornwall, but my father was Methodist, had been born in Wales, had been taken to Liverpool while a child, had grown to hate all things English and all things about his father and brothers, and who had come to the mines and fields for work, young. He had adopted the harsh local church's ways to such an extent that the locals called him Deacon, and on Sundays, would give fire and brimstone speeches, nearly stealing the pulpit from the local minister.

He believed that Hell lay in wait for all of us, for we had been baptized in what he called "The Devil's pagan church," his term for the Roman Catholic Church. He was certain that we all would die without resurrection, and that our mother, whom he claimed to love dearly, had already lost her mortal soul to the fires of Hell, but that his good Christian nature tried to redeem her throughout their lives together. He believed that Heaven was harder to get into than the local pub on a Saturday night. He typified the Welsh phrase: *Angel pen ffordd, a diawl pen tan. An angel abroad, a devil at home.*

Whereas he was an inspiration to the local congregation, and was considered one of the great local men of God (on Sundays, although he was well-ignored by the villagers the rest of the time), he was a cold, hard taskmaster to his children.

He used God to squelch us, and the threat of Hell to keep us silent. He continued his Methodist traditions within our family, and had named the first five of my siblings biblically. Thus, I had brothers Shadrac, Mishac, and Abednego, and two sisters, one named Sephera, and one, Bathsheba. I had escaped this fate when my mother insisted on naming me for her grandfather, who had recently died, and my twin, for my father's father.

My father's family was called ap Graver or sometimes Graver-Son (or Son of Graver, as my birth record reads: "Baptized this day, July, Iestyn, son of the Son of Graver"), and was from the ancient and country people, with peasants and yeomen in our ancestry, of Wales mixed with the conquering English. My father was a fallen son of a fallen son, which meant he had cousins and even brothers who had some wealth, but through a series of bad events, my father had no contact with them. He had been slothful (I can truthfully write now, but I could never think this when living under his roof), and had believed that one ought not to work for one's daily bread, but must convince others to pass their bread over for his convenience. My father, unlike my brothers and I, didn't worked the mines or the field. He was not a laborer, my mother would tell us, as she worked in peoples' homes and swept the alleyways behind the shops to make her pittance that supported all of us. My father was a ne'erdowell, and not of the romantic variety. His face was like a crazed eagle—the nose hooked, the eyes blue, the nostrils flared, and the filthy mop of hair across his forehead like some overgrown barleyfield

My mother was a martyr who refused to die—she lived through the deaths of four of her children, and worked any job she could find, still managed to say the rosary at the local church twice a day, and believed that Jesus Christ and the Virgin Mary had given her these burdens in order to prepare her for sainthood in the next life. I honestly believe she wanted to die, and be remembered for her Faith. Instead, the poor woman—whom I loved dearly, despite my talk of her—lived until she was 93, and saw all she loved destroyed, and all she feared, come to pass.

I was born when she was thirty-six, and my father was forty. My earliest memory was looking up at my mother's face, as I, at three, was still at her tit, nursing. She looked like the Virgin Mother to me then, and I remembered being disappointed when I could no longer drink that sacred milk.

In my generation was the beginning of my regeneration. In my fathers loins and my mother's womb, a mystery arrived to the world. I was not that mystery, but I was born with it. I was born in the year 1831, during a cholera epidemic, which was then simply called the Miasma. According to legend (for I heard of it years later), the Miasma swept through like a broom from Hell ("A Scourge!" my father shouted from the pulpit, no doubt), taking with it the breath of many children in our and other villages. The cities beyond us also were in its path, and many died during this time, particularly among the very young and the very old.

Mother Death (as the locals called her) spared me.

As I grew, I seemed to develop a taste for the morbid, and often went to the graveyard of the children who had died, feeling as if I somehow knew them better than children who were alive. I can't say for certain that this came from any particular event. It was simply something about death that drew me to it, rather than repulsed me.

My mother later told me the hand of God was upon me, and protected me from the Miasma.

But God was nowhere to be found for my twin. When I learned of his name and his death, I wept and was inconsolable. I had always felt a strange emptiness, as if I were only half a boy, as if I had another part of me that was somehow missing, as one is missing an arm or a leg—a phantom self that I had knowledge of, but knew not. It is difficult to express, but it was like knowing that one isn't completely alive. A lung that does not function. A nostril that cannot inhale and exhale breath. I felt that others had this, that my brothers and sister and friends in the mines and in the schoolhouse, all seemed whole. But

I did not. And when my mother told me about my dead twin, I knew why.

My twin died six months after we both were born. His name was Lloyd. I visited his little grave in the field beyond the village, sometimes weekly, and thought of how close I had gotten to Mother Death but she had, instead, chosen to suckle my brother. I sometimes attribute to my need for "the Other," and some of the unsuitable attachments I've made in my life, to the loss of that unknowable twin.

My only experience with the spirit world as a child came while I sat by my twin's grave. I wasn't then sure of what it meant, if it was anything at all. I just heard someone say the words, "Carry me to the water, look, and know the truth."

5

Carry me to the water? Know the truth? These words seemed too profound to have come just from my childish mind.

And yet, more than anything, I wanted to know. I wanted to know my twin in some way. I wanted to understand what, even then, I considered a mystical experience.

I went to my older sister, Bathsheba, who was my only true confidante among my siblings. She was sixteen, and ready to be married, and in some ways had been more my mother than our mother had been. I asked her about this strange voice, and she told me that I should ignore such things.

"These are demons of ill omen," she said, for she had become a staunch puritan in her beliefs, influenced as she was by our father. "Do not go to those graves. Your brother is not sanctified."

Then, she told me the story of how, the night my brother had died, our father buried him quickly, and in the night, embarrassed that the child had neither been baptized nor saved in any outward way. She had been five years old at the time, and she had asked our mother why she must not mention her dead brother again.

Our mother had told her, "God has taken him. Let God keep his secrets."

As Bathsheba explained it to me, there were demons and terrible spirits that lurked among the graves, and I should not wander there, nor seek solace at my twin's side. "The Lord Jesus wishes you to seek salvation only," she said. I was young enough to half-believe her words, although I doubted that my brother was surrounded by demons, for if he were my twin, he slept with angels.

The voice, and these words, haunted me. Perhaps it was God, I thought, or just a voice that might arise in my head now and then. But I had the distinct impression that it was a voice I had never before heard, and, because I sat by the baby's grave, I attributed it to him.

The grave was one of several, where the babies were buried, called, in Welsh, the Baban Claddfa, from the old days, and it was on a hillside overlooking a slender river that ran for several miles.

I didn't know why the voice bade me carry it to the river.

I felt it was my brother, though how a baby dead many years would learn the English language and speak from heaven as a much older child, I had no notion.

The Necromancer

I let this incident go by the wayside, although I mentioned it to my mother, who suggested that it might be the Virgin, despite the fact that it sounded like the voice of a boy who was very much my own age.

When, finally, vexed by the memory of this voice, I went one morning, in the mud of spring, to truly see for myself what this voice might've meant.

Chapter Two
A Mystery of Bones

1

I took my father's tools, and dug the grave as if it were a rose needing to be replanted. I found the bundle only a few feet down in the earth (for it was the custom, particularly in the rocky soil, to keep shallow graves on the hillsides, for, with other years to come, graves were often moved to various locations, or else disinterred altogether and taken to a common grave after considerable time had passed.) This was surely a morbid task for me to undertake, but I had spent too many nights wanting to see his bones, to see what I would have been, had I died so young, and to fulfill this request that I could not get free from in my mind.

When I opened the bundle, I saw what seemed to me the bones of a bird. His small dessicated corpse, the darkened thin leather of skin stuck to bone. I cradled my twin in my arms and whispered to him that I hoped he was in heaven.

Then, I carried the bundle to the river, and sat down on the rocks, holding it. There was a shallow, quiet edge to the narrow river, rounded by stones placed there by the girls who came with their morning's washing. It was a bowl of still water, surrounded by the gently moving current around the stones. It was this that I would use for my baptismal font. I peered into the dark water, and saw my reflection, and how well I remember it, my small, boy-face, the sadness in my eyes, and the sense that someone stood there with me, peering down at my reflection as well. I turned around quickly, but there was no one near me, or up on the hillside, even.

I waited, wondering if his voice would come, but it did not.

It occurred to me that my brother had never been baptized. Perhaps this, I thought, was what the voice intended, the truth at the river I was meant to find.

So, I leaned over and cupped my free hand in the water, and brought it up to the skull. I poured the icy water over it, saying things that sounded suitably Biblical to me, a mix of words remembered from both the Catholic and Methodist services.

Again, I looked at my reflection, and felt as if there were something momentous about to happen, some faerie would come up from the water, perhaps, or God would offer a sign. But there was nothing. Just my face, wan and with that hungry look that poor boys have.

I held my brother's remains in my arms, cradling him the way our mother surely must have done.

And that is when I saw that the back edge of the skull had been crushed.

2

It wasn't a large hole that had been made in his skull, but fairly small, as if some tool had been used. The bone of the skull was cracked around it, and it was just big enough for me to press my finger into it.

Not knowing what to make of this, at least at that moment, I stared at it awhile longer. I began to think about the Miasma that had come through when I'd been a baby, and imagined my brother Lloyd growing sicker soon after he was born. I had heard that surgeons sometimes did horrible things, and had seen a man who had a hole in his head from where a surgeon had to drill in order to relieve pressure. The man lived in our village, and did not seem worse for his cranial opening. Perhaps, I thought, my little brother had been sick, but the physician called to help might have tried some measure to relieve his pain or suffering. Perhaps. I didn't completely believe this, nor did I, then, want to find out the truth.

But it gnawed at me.

Thus, when I was ten years' old, I discovered how secrets are kept, and how they are often buried, and yet refuse to remain underground.

3

My brother had been killed. Perhaps accidentally. But killed, nonetheless. By whom? I could guess, but I could not know for sure. Nor could I find out, because I would not know who to trust to ask.

Someone had bashed his small head in, and then had not even had the decency to baptize him at the local church after death (which was sometimes done.)

Because, if he were baptized, a priest might notice the skull. It would be known that it was not the Miasma, but murder. I knew that my dead brother's message to me was about saving me from his murderer, and avenging his death. There was a monster in our house, and he was my father.

You may think it morbid of me, the little boy with the baby's bones in his hands, but I wrapped the bones carefully and then hid them in a hollow of a tree. I covered over his grave, even going so far as to dig up patches of grass and press it into the muddy earth to make it seem as if it had not been disturbed. While I did this, I had the peculiar sense of being watched, but as was true at the river, no one seemed to be nearby.

At first, I kept my brother's bones in the tree for weeks, and then, one night, I took them under my shirt and ragged coat, and brought them home. I shared a room with my brothers, so it was not easy to hide anything in the house, but we had an outhouse in the back, shared with several other families, and behind the seat, there was an area where rags were kept. I laid the bones well under the rags, and checked on my brother regularly, speaking to the bones as if they could hear me, telling him what I was thinking, and of my dreams and ambitions.

I went on this way, between work and school and home and the bones of my brother, for several years.

I held the conviction that my father, who was prone to violent outbursts and believed in the whipping post and the rod, was the murderer of my twin. I watched him carefully, and avoided him when I could.

The Necromancer

As time passed, my sister Bathsheba married a local boy who worked at the mill, and in the mornings, as a baker. My older brothers eventually began to seek their fortunes beyond the walls of our small home. I became, in the home, the eldest, and I clung to the uncomfortable safety of the room I shared with my younger brothers, nearly afraid of the future that awaited me, of a life of ash and coal, but also wanting to protect my brothers and sisters from my father's wrath. We clashed often, my father and I. More than once I had to shout at him for pummeling my younger siblings for some imagined sin or crime. As a result, I often took a beating myself in their stead.

Thoughts of Lloyd kept me up at night. Of the bones. Of the skull.

4

Victoria had been on the throne since I'd been six, and perhaps it was my rebellion against anything approaching propriety that got me to become a bit wild, compared to the other boys my age, who seemed beaten down by the mines and the ashy life we were forced to live.

I ran to pleasure whenever I could, whether it was candy or clotted cream or the bodies of the local girls. I truly loved pleasure, and as I got older, the pleasures became more enticing.

I lost my physical virginity at sixteen to a factory girl in Newcastle, whose thighs seemed so big around that I got lost inside her for minutes at a time.

Chapter Three
The Discovery of Sex and the Rite of Manhood

1

She smothered me with her affections and her affectations, no doubt expecting marriage and a life away from the sooty skies and endless hours of working in a dark coal basement by the light of sulphur, her lungs growing blacker and her heart growing weary, even in her early 20s. She was pretty, for a poor girl, as I was perhaps handsome for a poor boy, and we found our pleasure by meeting in the woods and sheep meadows behind the shambling manor house on the hillside. It was a dangerous meeting, for many a boy had had an ear cut off for wandering on the landowner's property, but because it was early spring, the master of the house was still off in distant London, and the youth of the area often dallied there, finding the moist warmth of wench and whore and ambitious girl in the tall grasses, or against a rock, or behind the old stone wall overlooking the paddock. I recall now that she grunted and moaned and swore like a boatswain in a brothel when I brought my greater self into her, and she clutched me around the middle and whispered obscenities that would've made a whore blush.

This was my first rite of my manhood, and was the chief pleasure of one who worked from four in the morning until eight at night from the age of eight years onward, and was the only happy moment of my life at home. Pleasure, physical pleasure, taught me that there was more to the world than what I had known. The stroking, the rocking, the gentle tug of war between her skin and mine, the lapping of tongues and the wet feeling between us, and within my own body, the building of pressure into an explosion…it is not a subject that the world speaks much of, but for those of us who are born to want, it is the first we know that within our own beings, we can create our own worlds. The flesh itself provides knowledge, entertainment, craft, and heaven.

Pleasure led me to pleasure.

My next chief pleasure became learning.

I learned about physical pleasure then, but books were more my calling. I self-taught myself to read by quizzing the local schoolmistress, and eventually seducing her as well. She was not more than two years my senior, nonetheless, and we had bouts of pleasure in bed, on the floor, against the schoolroom wall, and she taught me what I had not been able to learn in many years of our one-room schoolhouse. She brought me great books, and Latin Primers. She met my thrusts with declarations taken from Shakespeare and Marlowe. We sweated against each other, making ungodly noises that

The Necromancer

would surely make the angels weep, as I made her read me *Paradise Lost*. This was my earliest blasphemy, for we moved onto the original Italian of Dante's *Inferno*, and I was never not inside her body as she taught me that foreign tongue with her own tongue.

My love of England grew as she cupped me in her hands and whispered sonnets and lusty ballads of medieval origin in my ear.

2

In the meantime, I managed to work the mines fewer hours, and instead took in shoemaking and clock-fixing work, as I was fairly mechanically-inclined, and found a burning within me to learn more, do more, make more money, find more pleasure. I found pleasure in things outside the bedroom, in whatever new that I could learn, whatever theory I could grasp. I borrowed books on physics and naturalism from the manor's library, whose master had begun to enjoy my company as I repaired his mistress' boot, or worked on the great clock in his grand hall.

My sexual companion, whom I shall, for discretion's sake, call Miss French, or Bootsy, as I called her for the peculiarly tromping but elegant ladies' boot she wore, didn't like my other work. She felt that I should be available to her for her pleasure and to assuage her never-quenched loneliness.

Eventually, we tired of each other, for I had learned more from her than she had from me, and the scandal came out—from her own mouth, for she could not refrain from boasting to her sewing circle that she regularly trapped the most handsome youth in our little village and intended to marry him once she was with child. These were not enlightened times, and although every schoolboy knew of the factory girls and their easy ways, we had fire and brimstone on Sundays and were taught that our lower regions were tools of Satan, who longed to misguide us and condemn us to eternal perdition.

It was a horrifying moment for me, to walk into our hovel, and have my mother slap me for "that devilry," and for my father to want to throw me, bodily, from the house. In some families, fathers might be proud of their son's swordsmanship, but my father was puritanical and harsh to each of us, and believed we were the stain of sin for his having married someone not Methodist "of the Roman scourge," as he called the Catholic Church. We children were mongrels, unworthy of salvation, unworthy of anything but lifelong penitence.

My father and I began fighting, arguing, throwing chairs, of which we had few to spare, and cursing at each other. My mother sat in the corner and wept as my father chastised me for my ways, and I crowed about wanting to leave this graveyard of a home. Finally, I drew out my trump card.

The bones themselves would speak.

3

I dashed through the back window, and ran to the outhouse. Digging through the rags, I picked up the bundle of my brother's bones and sped straight away back into the house, like a monkey leaping tree to tree. I held the small sack up, crowing, "I know what happened to Lloyd!"

My father put his hands on his hips, eyeing me with suspicion. "What are you yapping about?"

The Necromancer

"What you did! What you did to him! My brother. My twin brother. I know it wasn't the Miasma!" With this I opened the sack, and poured my brother out onto the hearthstone, near my mother who screamed when she saw it, and although I had some remorse for this overly dramatic revelation, I felt it was the moment that needed to happen. The truth had to come out! I had to throw in their faces what I had known and what I had kept secret for several years.

"And what is it you think you know, you worthless whelp?" His voice had quieted a bit, but was like an incision in a fresh wound: sharp and painful and precise. "What is it you think you've discovered?"

"Dear God!" my mother cried out, of a sudden. "He died of the Miasma. It was terrible. Dear God in heaven!" Her sobs were now peppered with little shrieks of agony, the like of which I had never before heard from anyone.

"No," I said, feeling triumphant to finally bring this to light. "He didn't. You knew it." I pointed at my father as a judge to the convicted. "You killed him. You bashed his head in. You murdered my brother! You didn't even have the decency to baptize him! You buried him in secret, in the night! You monster!"

My father shook his head, glaring at me all the while. "You fool," he spat. "Is this how you repay your mother for caring for you, for cleaning you, for feeding you? Is this how you repay us for giving you food and shelter and a Christian upbringing?"

"You're a monster!" I shouted at him, pointing my finger as if laying a curse.

"Look at you," he said. "Look at you, grave-digging, stirring things up, lifting the skirts of the local whores and ruining girls, generating bastards for all we know. You, my boy, are the monster."

My mother's weeping increased, and she covered her face with her hands. Through her heaving sobs, I heard her say the Hail Mary.

Then, monstrously, my father began laughing, roaring loud. "You want to know what happened to your twin? You want to know why he is in that grave, and you are not?" Then, turning to my mother, he said, "Why don't you tell him, my love. Why don't you let your son know why he is alive and his twin lies in the graves of the Angels?"

I looked at my mother, but her face was covered, and her weeping, copious. I was torturing her with this, I felt. I had not wanted to reach this position of uncorking the family vintage, of raising my brother's death and its mystery, but I had done so, nonetheless. Her heartache was readily apparent, and I realized I was the curse of the household.

I did not belong there anymore.

What surprised me the most in all this was that my father did not raise his hand against me. I almost had the feeling that he was frightened of me now.

I went to embrace my mother, but her trembling body seemed unwelcoming. I gathered up my brother's bones, as many as I could quickly grab, including his skull and ribcage, and put them in the sack.

My father had calmed, although his eyes smoldered as he watched me.

"I am leaving. For good," I said.

My father bid me good riddance, saying I was far too old to be sharing their roof anyway, that my older

The Necromancer

brothers had left at fourteen and I should have followed their examples and that I had brought heartache and damnation into his home.

I left, with my mother's sobs like a banshee's wail, following me along the streets of the village.

I thought of Lloyd, the small bones in the sack bundle, and the chips of his gentle barely-formed skull pushed in, smashed. I felt confused by my father's taunting, but my mother's tears had been unequivocal. That my father had killed him seemed certain. Or did it? Had my mother, perhaps, murdered him? Why had my father laughed at mention of his death? My mind conjured possibilities: that my mother, with two babies still nursing, and now twins, that she had not enough milk to go around. Or perhaps she had been sick after our births, and had dropped my brother, or again, the thought that a surgeon had been called to relieve some pressure on his brain. Why had my father laughed? What monster would laugh when remembering the death of his child?

I had no answers, still.

Whatever had happened to my brother would remain a mystery, for I would abandon the family of my birth, and seek my fortune in the world.

Chapter Four
A New Life

1

I had nothing, and no one. Even my schoolmistress would not take me, for I was now not good enough for the likes of her, though she had been painted with the Whore of Babylon's powder brush. At midnight, I banged on the door of the baker's shop, over which my sister Bathsheba, her husband, and my niece, slept. Bathsheba came out eventually, and told me that Jesus would guide me, that I needed to give my soul over to the Lord and to repent of my sins.

"You do not know what you do now," she said. "You believe you understand the world and its forces, but you have followed the ways of the flesh. You must repent, and look to the word of God. Forsake this carnal pastime, and make a scourge of your flesh." She had recited my father's words so much that they were her normal way of speaking.

"You are the godforsaken," I told her, and left her there, in the dark of her doorway with these final words, "You will come to know the Devil yourself one day, and your Lord will not pluck you from his fiery arms."

I was nearly eighteen, and without a place to sleep.

2

That night, I slept on the high summer grass, and stared up at the stars, or what could be seen of them, for, even at night, the black smoke roiled in the heavens.

I spoke aloud to God, unsure if my youthful nature would keep him deaf to my pleas.

But I had an answer by morning, as to my question of what I should do next.

The railroad industry was growing rapidly and had been since my birth. The news of railway races, testing their speed and comfort, came to us weekly from Liverpool and Manchester. The plans of expanding the rails to all parts of the British Isles filled my dreams with exploration. On the continent, great changes occurred as well, and it all made me believe that we were entering a new phase of human existence, when nothing could not be touched, seen, experienced. I wanted to be part of it. The industry around the rails was about to grow, and there were jobs to the north and east. Industries must advance, and I knew that I had talents with numbers and an engineering sense, as well as my newfound knowledge of literature and the past, that could be applied to this new world within the old world that would mean something important for me. We were entering more fully the Age of Machines, and I knew it was my opportunity to build a fortune.

The Necromancer

At the mines in Newcastle, we'd had railway-like trams for mining, and I had repaired them at times, and knew many aspects of their engineering which even the older men did not know. I knew I could somehow make my way in the world with the newer, more modern railways that would carry passengers long distances. I had an Uncle in Manchester, so I'd been told, though I had never met him. I would somehow get there, sleep in his shed, and work in some capacity. I was good with numbers, and now had a decent education in English, with a smattering of Latin and Italian. Surely, I could find better work than shoveling coal or shearing sheep.

So, I set off, walking, hitching rides with the less reputable carriage lines, sleeping beneath bridges, feeling, as one does at that age, the freedom of life. The freedom from family. The sense that the world is about to open up for you as you discover it.

The belief that it is a benevolent dictator, this life.

3

So I left all I had known, begged, borrowed, and stole my way to my uncle's. When passing through a large enough town, and having no money to speak of, I went to the local Anglican church, which would have a comfortable chapel. I would go in and sleep on the pews until such a time in the morning I would be thrown out. In one such town, I was thrown from the premises early, and went to sleep among the graves. I brought out my brother's bones, and, finding a fresh grave that had not yet been filled with its tenant, buried my brother at the bottom of the newly dug plot, and covered this over with sod.

Lloyd had a Christian burial at last, at least in terms of location. Both my father and mother would think this a blasphemy, as they each believed the Anglicans were the most corrupt of all the heathen churches.

I slept well, atop the grave of a former magistrate of the town, and when I awoke, the local priest found me there and offered me a fine breakfast and three pounds from the poorbox to help me on my way to my uncle's home.

4

My uncle lived in the heart of Manchester, an industrial town that was growing and full of possibilities, at least to me and the hundreds that flocked there. Although others might call it dirty and boring, I found the streets of Manchester to be like the firmament itself: it was wall to wall possibility, and sometimes, that is all a young man with less than a penny in his pocket and a talent for fixing things needs.

Uncle Meyrick was now called Maurice, had taken the last name Gravesend, as was the fashion then (to modify a name that sounded too old-fashioned or perhaps even of a lower caste, it was becoming the norm to Anglify it as completely as possible.) So, I too, became, not Iestyn ap Graver, but Justin Gravesend, and with the name adjustment, felt as if a whole new life were offered, with a whole new teat from which to suck.

My Uncle Maurice lived in a hulking cottage that was made up of two rooms, with a kitchen in a separate small house outside. He welcomed me like the prodigal son. He had a heart as big as the city itself, and I knew my luck had changed when we met and he embraced me

The Necromancer

as if he had been waiting his whole life to see one of his nephews. He made some choice words about my father and mother, and then told me to go and bathe and he would buy me some new clothes for my new life. When I had clean-shaven and sponged myself in an ill-fitting tub, he returned with clothes that, to me, seemed spun from gold, yet they were ordinary work clothes of the time.

Uncle Maurice was a jovial drunk with a wide pink face and an excellent way about him that made few women love him but many men adore his company. He was a raconteur who enjoyed brandy and cigars, and had learned to cheat at cards without offending his partners. He made his living by running a tobacco and sundries shop near the waterfront, and he lived part off this, and part from a yearly allowance from the estate of his great-grandfather, from which my family had been disinherited. He was generous to a fault, and I grew to love him as my own father. He introduced me to men at the railyard, who tested me for keeping books for the railway, and soon, I was earning my keep and contributing to my uncle's household. I even managed to send a little money each month to my mother, worried about her cough (of which she'd written me) and that she might put some savings aside for her old age. Now and then, my sister Bathsheba would write to me and tell me how badly I'd treated our father, and how God wished for me to return to Him so that I might understand my sinful ways. I ignored her letters, and would send her brief notes telling her that I was happy to hear about her latest child, my new nephew or niece, and I included a few pennies for the child's upkeep. I held no animosity toward her, for I considered

Bathsheba a lost soul in that horrible village, stuck in a life I had so gladly escaped. My other brothers and sisters fared better, and got far away, some of them even going to America, others to jobs in the Midlands, where new industries were just being born.

I enjoyed these several months, but before I was nineteen, Uncle Maurice warned me that I shan't want to be adding numbers in a ledger book my whole life. "You need more than this. Just, you have a mind that's better than your beginnings."

He meant for me to enter the university, and so I submitted to the barrage of tests and entrance examinations, primarily oral, to attend. I failed some of them, but impressed the faculty enough that I was allowed two courses of study to begin. I had a talent with biology, particularly regarding human anatomy, which I could only attribute to my many hours gazing at my brother's bones. So, I was to study the natural world with seminars in anatomy and physiology, and literature, although I would not end up as either a surgeon or professor, two vocations that seemed to require a wealthy family in order to rise within the ranks.

Within weeks, I had added more studies, and attended class in the mornings, and worked the ledger books at night. My new classes included botany and biology, as well as astronomy, when time permitted. I began reading the new books then being published: the works of the American Nathaniel Hawthorne, Charles Dickens' *The Personal History of David Copperfield*, and Alfred, Lord Tennyson's, *In Memorium*, which affected me greatly. It was a world that was so different from the blackened skies of my childhood that I felt, at times, like I had died

The Necromancer

and gone to heaven. I found there was more to learn than my ardent schoolmistress had even suspected.

Despite the roiling of the world's events, news from America and the Continent of upheavals, and even the news from London, I hid from the world, into the literature I could find. The languages I could learn. Pages I turned until my fingers nearly bled, and my eyes blurred. I ignored the physical and grew a bit fat around the belly, but soon learned to fast and keep from gaining the odd stone or two by restricting my diet to a near-prisoner's fare. I added boxing to my repertoire of exercise, as well as a then popular athletic game called Rugby that I'd been taught by the rich boys at my college who seemed to spend most of their days in lackadaisical pursuits and narcissistic rituals. I admired them, to some extent, for their inability or interest in making money. They had no need of it, for they were the sons of estates and landowners and they were at university merely to pass the time before they'd return to the manor houses of their boyhood and work the tenants to their deaths. They spoke of war as if it were an extension of their favorite sports, and they had no fear of the future. Nor did they have a sense that it held possibilities. In this, I felt bad for them. Additionally, I felt a bit of grief when they spoke of our college, for they were the low end of their schools—their fellows and siblings had gone on to better universities, while they were stuck in Manchester, not quite bright enough to make it to Oxford. I, myself, felt that Manchester was the peak of the kind of education I could get, and it had more to offer than I believe these fellows knew.

While there, I read every piece of literature, learned Latin and French and German and Russian. I studied politics and the law. I found myself with nosebleeds from staying up all night several days in a row in order to keep working and keep studying. I was motivated by a sheer desire to never return to the factories and the coal pits and the farmlands and the stink of sheep and the taste of two-day-old kidney pie or cold porridge or mutton stew left too long in the pot.

I wanted a finer life, and so I avoided more entanglements of the flesh, sure that some comely but desperate lass would pull down her underthings and press herself onto my engorged pole in order to saddle me with children and a bleak future. I had seen it happen often enough to other boys from the colliery.

I wanted to be as far away from the black skies of my childhood as possible, and away from the father who threw me against walls to keep me silent, and the mother who thought I would go to hell if I spoke one word against my father, as if he were Jesus Christ himself. I knew that there were people with money, the men who owned the mines, who owned the lands, whose sons went to Eton and Harrow and Darlington Rows, schools where the skies were clean and no one sickened from daily living, and those boys would go on to Oxford and Cambridge and the world's universities, or were beside me at Manchester, while I, and my kind, would enter the dark mines and bring up the coal to heat the rich man's homes.

I wanted to live their lives, and stay far from the one in which I had been dumped, like ash in a bin.

The Necromancer

And so, I finished my studies early, having been one of the most brazen and unstoppable of students, driven to master language and history and oratory, and become more than a keeper of figures and numbers, and move into the realm of which the rich boys I knew had no regard simply because it meant nothing to them: I wanted to be a master of the world.

5

When I was twenty-one, I lost my spiritual virginity, when I met a man I shall call the Necromancer, who took me by the hand and led me down pathways into the human and eternal mind, and introduced me to the mystical union of those who influence the Earth, the Planets, and the Cosmos.

And he taught me about Sex Magick for the first time.

Visionary 2

My manhood grows long and fat, and begins to speak from its narrow mouth, and tell of the pain that is inflicted upon it when it is used to bring forth life. Then, I see it is merely my phallus again, engorged, and I find the one who offers a portal for me, a doorway to enter and then seal the entrance again, my sacrifice who has ingested the herb and whose glassy eyes turn toward me, lips parted slightly, between a gasp and a prayer and love.

I press myself there, feel the dry warmth, and I call the names of my kindred, my brethren, to bear witness to the lightning that I shall bring into myself, into the tomb where we meet, through the altar of the one who has offered to me the most sacred vessel.

The jackals of that other realm begin to howl for their meat, who still writhes in my arms as I beat myself into that world, the very geometry of my flesh expanding outward, as it webs and stretches, reaching like a mollusk's foot to touch the sandy bottom of some new sea.

Chapter Five
London Adventure

1

During the spring after my 21st birthday, some of the rich young students, who had so recently seemed like boys to me but were now gentlemen, invited me to go with them down to London. These were boys who had paid no attention to me in the early years of my study, for I was poor, and spoke as a poor boy and dressed as a poor boy. I was from the rustic gutter, in their opinion, and no matter how well I learned the finer turns of phrases, no matter how my uncle's old clothes fit me well, and no matter that my income from working the accounting books on the rails in the city put pound notes in my pocket, I was somehow lesser.

There was no way around this issue of class, and it continues on into the world, but in my youth, it was at its worse.

The boys who were only just becoming men sneered and strutted, and yet were great fun in their own ways. But they never let me forget my station, and when I saw their servants, who often brought them tea in the common rooms of the university, I realized that my status in life might even be beneath their butlers and maids. And yet, through my limited wit and basic intelligence and no doubt their own natural curiosity about a rustic who got top marks, these rich boys gradually warmed to me, and eventually, two of them spent more and more time with me at the local ale-house, which was slumming for them.

"You're a jolly fellow," one said to me, one evening, downing a pint. "You aren't like the others."

"No, you're not," his chum said. "I suppose its not true what they say about colliers and their brains—being blackened with soot."

This passed for wit, and, wanting to get along, I laughed with them, then drank with them, and eventually awoke on the floor of their rooms, feeling as if I, too, were a gentleman. Or, at the very least, passing for one. I was vain and foolish, of course, but I was young and wanting a better life. Their acceptance meant the world to me.

One of my new friends said something that I couldn't possibly understand at the time, but which seemed important. I heard him, in the next room, door open, say to his friend, "It's hard to believe it's this one."

"True," the other said. "But I was there. I heard it said."

At the time, this just seemed like idle conversation between them, and I didn't make anything of it.

The Necromancer

2

It is pathetic to think this now, but at the time, I wanted to be part of that larger world, the one that would put me as far away from the coalfields as possible. And I felt that I was moving in that direction. With these newfound friends, perhaps I would get there.

3

It was April, and I'd been studying too hard, pouring over Latin texts and trying to decipher the medical books I'd just found, dealing with aspects of the human body. Learning about the physical of the body was the most discouraging part of my education, and after doing so, I wished I had remained ignorant, and happy.

I found myself drawn to medicine, perhaps not as practice, but as an area of serious study. I gained access, through professors who believed I would be a credit to them, to the great arenas of the medical school.

I watched as corpses were opened and revealed. It soured my stomach to the smells of the human body, dead or alive, and, fascinated though I was by the human reproductive organs, I did not enjoy seeing them under the carving knife of the local physician whom I passed daily on the streets.

Watching the scientific evisceration of the human corpse made me wonder if all human life was not just some shit-stink of existence with nothing to redeem it. After all, where was God for the body at the center of the room? That man, or woman, had not risen from the dead to ascend into heaven.

That corpse was just meat on a table, to be flayed and filleted and shanked and cut into morsels for the surgeons in attendance, and the curious students, such as myself. It was a butcher shop of humanity, and I could not see in the scissors and saws of the professors of medicine, whose aprons were brown from the blood of countless operations, whose instruments were thick with the congealed blood and bits of hair of the many who had died beneath their learned care, God—anywhere. God or Christ or the Virgin. Merely the utter waste and futility of all human endeavor.

This is what we come to, I thought. My youthful dreams of glory and wealth were nothing, because they would not prolong my life, they would not reduce misery, they would not turn the tide of the greatest problem of all human existence, which is that the only Queen of Heaven (or Hell or Earth) is Mother Death, Mater Mort, Persephone in her matronly aspect, gobbling pomegranate seeds while she raises her fingernails to slice at the hearts of humankind, throwing back her head to laugh at all human ambition and desire.

Even Uncle Maurice and his young wife (whom he'd just met and married the previous winter) recognized my newfound despondency and perhaps a morbid turn of mind from all the hours of study and examination. Uncle Maurice felt I needed an interlude before my final few courses were complete. "You're a young man. Being young doesn't last forever. Go enjoy April. Meet some fine women. Drink, rest, see the world a bit," he told me. How he could possibly have come from the same family that had produced my father, I still, to this day, can't fathom. He was the most generous soul, and loving. He was a man among men, happy with his lot, constant in his affection, and never felt that the world was anything but a wonderful place.

The Necromancer

I had avoided the pleasures of life in favor of the pleasures of the brain, which I found could have no equal, so I thought, in human relations. But I took the advice, even accepting a few quid from my uncle, and managed to get, through my employer, free fares for my two schoolchums on the rails that would take us to the great city, which I had not yet seen. I had learned that very rich young men expected to be given things for free.

"Prepare to be humbled," Wendy, short for Wendell, the older of the two told me, crushing a ten pound note into my hand, which seemed like a fortune as the train slowly entered the city proper. "Now, run and get us some libation from the platform, will you? I have an enormous thirst."

We drank much, laughed much, slept, and nearly missed a connection at one point. We ate too many watercress and butter sandwiches at a small station buttery when we had a two hour delay between trains.

It was our fourth train on the voyage that had seemed long, and in between trains, we had to catch hansoms to make our connection. I was weary and bleary-eyed, and ready to just sleep when he said, "This is London. This is the place for all-hours' debauchery."

Always an avid sport for debauchery, or so I thought, I imagined beautiful women, magnificent clubs, and smart men with brilliant ideas. I regained my energies and felt renewed as we entered the station.

My first sight of the city had confirmed what I'd read of it in books: it was the center of the growing empire, and seemed to me like Rome in its ancient glory.

But like Rome, it had its filth and squalor.

4

When we left the train, and went to find a hansom, I saw nothing but a cesspool. The train station itself was fashionably kept, but just beyond it began what seemed a human swamp of misery and carelessness, its stench like the terrible river. The sky was not clear, but had become nearly as blackened as the sky of my home. It was a city of greatness and despair, like twins holding hands, one dead, one living, one failing, one advancing. I did not like it at all, and had to be convinced by my companions that there was more to this New Rome than met the eye.

Once further into town, the beauty of it came about again, the palaces and grand apartments, the boulevards and parks, all of which I'd studied. Apartments that seemed like palaces lined the beautiful boulevards, great white buildings and skies above that faded from black to pale blue. It was as if we'd stepped from a museum gallery in which all the paintings were of lepers, into one in which the pantheon of Greek gods suddenly appeared. My companions pointed out the fashionable clubs, the houses of great ladies and gentlemen—many I knew from reading the newspapers, but none of whom seemed human to me, for they were beyond the rabble of mankind I had known all my life. Statesmen and great novelists and war heroes and legendary actors—all living within several blocks of each other, in this mansion of a city that we toured as we went up to my friend's London home.

But I could not shake those first things I'd seen outside the train station. They put the poverty that hovered in parts of Manchester to shame. They put the hopelessness of Cwthshire and its ash heaps to shame, as well. That this grand whore of a city could have festering syphilitic wounds like this, that on her painted face, a gilded beauty, and her gown was the finest silk, but still tinged with mud at the ragged hem, and beneath her great skirts, dirty underclothes, and fistulas in her private parts from decay and disease.

And yet, James and Wendy brought me to a fine townhouse opposite the Regent's Park, where the sound of carriages arriving, the shiny horses that seemed to have finer lives than the poor of the city, and the laughter of fine young ladies seemed worlds away from the filthy undergarments from which we'd entered. The place was full of servants, some of whom were there to draw the bath, to dress us, to bring us drink, to coddle us in every way that a man is not meant to be coddled. Curiously, the servants were all beautiful, both the women and the men. The men were young and strong with the features of gods, and the women were of heart-shaped face and large-bosom, and seemed like beautiful statues brought to life to do the bidding of the rich. It was as if the rich only hired the cream of the crop in terms of looks, breeding, and character. Or so I thought at the moment I was introduced to the employees of the house. One particular maid caught my eye—she was a slip of a girl of nineteen, but looked as if she could've been the subject of a great painter, like Vermeer. A young manservant had a face as white as dove's wings, and spoke a better class of the English language than even I could muster. I felt I should serve both of them tea and shine their shoes, for these servants were truly my betters.

No wonder my school chums had seemed so soft and tender—they had nothing to do other than explore pleasure and mischief and whatever they could dream up. They had no reason not to do as they pleased. I envied them, and yet felt bad that they had not ever done anything by and for themselves. It was as if, despite their youth and minds and athletic abilities, they were helpless babies in the crib.

And yet, there was immense beauty and possibility in their world, as well. To be bathed by a maidservant pouring warm water down your back, while a manservant scrubs your feet—that was as if I had died and gone to heaven—but to add to this a beautiful young lady at the harp, just beyond the bath, playing soothing dulcet tones on those strings had me wishing that I'd been born to this life rather than to the other one, of struggle and harsh words.

I am sad to say that I soon forgot that darker part of London, and instead, like my companions, bathed and made ready for a night on the town. I could easily take on the life of a fop, if given half the chance.

5

Drunk by six, having Madeira and something they called "Malmsey," I wobbled and laughed too easily and seemed far, far too joyous and excited—"Like a farmboy!" James slapped me on the back, having emerged from his bath half-naked and dripping on the floors of his great-aunt Minnie's house, a pure white confection that might've been a wedding cake. He told me, briefly, the house's history, how it was bought from a dissolute rich French cleric named Alphonse Constant, and thus was called "Constant House," by James' family, who renovated it within the past decade. He looked at me as if he realized his family history lesson was a bit of a bore. "You drink much more and you shall be sick."

"I shan't be sick, because I am too well," I said, not certain of my own logic.

"We are due at dinner at half past," James commanded, rapping on the door for Wendy, who had napped. He turned back to me, a broad smile on his face. "You've never met society ladies, have you?"

"Not that I'm aware," I said.

"Well, the protocol is set. Wen and I are the third tier suitors in their world, and they are a class above us in many ways." He said this all with a serious air.

"There is actually a class above you?"

He snorted with laughter. "They think so. They have more money and better blood. But we have charm. We entertain them, allow them to charm us, we charm them, and then, afterward, all the men go to the drawing room or, in this case, the library, for important talk."

"Sounds dreadful."

"It can be. But it's necessary for the evening's entertainment. Say, you'll need to dress better for these ladies." He went through the giant wardrobe in the room that he claimed had always been his, since childhood. He began throwing shirts and shoes and trousers all around the floor. I watched his disregard for the fabrics, for the exquisitley tailored clothes, and nearly wept.

"Whatever's the matter, old boy? Why so glum?"

"I...I just think they're beautiful. And too good for me."

"Clothes? These clothes? These are nearly ready for the rubbish heap," he said.

But I had never seen such fine clothing in my life, all in one wardrobe.

"Your Aunt Minnie won't like all this mess," I said, chiding him.

"Minnie lives here by my good graces. She has an allowance that comes from my father's estate, and if she isn't good to me, she is out on her bum. She knows this is my home first, hers second." He said it all breezily, as if the welfare of his great-aunt were simply a whim. Going through all the stiff white shirts, and hanging collars, he drew one out and threw it to me. "That about should fit you, and here," he said, a pair of dark trousers sailing my way, landing on my head. "If those don't quite fit, we can pinch them in with a hatpin or something."

I dove into the clothes, and felt every inch a rich gentleman just holding them in my hands. Two servants were called in to help me dress, which, for better or worse, aroused my "sleeping soldier," as James called it. But this was the strangest sensation of pleasure I'd ever experienced: to be touched simply while being dressed, as if I needed a staff of two to make sure all buttonhooks were fastened, cuffs and collar in place. It excited me just to feel that power over someone else. And I felt guilty, as well, for this way of living seemed wrong. I imagined my mother and father in their home, patching together clothes, sewing into the night, taking charity from the church to make sure they had enough blankets in the winter. Yet, I suppose, being a young man, and prone to pleasure and idleness, I was able to dismiss my guilt and my thoughts of my own beginnings. I was in a different milieu now.

James offered me quick lessons in etiquette: the knives, the forks, the way to eat peas, the way to slice the meat, and then added, "You'll meet several eligible young girls. You are not to mention snooker, only billiards. Nothing of rugby—too uncouth. You must not talk of Manchester, for it will bore them. Instead..." he paused, conjuring a thought. "Well, see here, Justy, they want to be wooed. Listen to their gossip, nod your head when they feel they have a point to make about which neighborhood has become less fashionable. They'll adore you, I daresay. Do not give in to the temptation to make love to them. They will consider you beneath them. They are looking for suitable catches. You are not one for them—now, don't be hurt. You don't want these girls. None of them are pretty in the least. They're rather plain, in fact. Plain but rich."

"Don't you find this charade despicable?"

He raised an eyebrow, considering. "Not in the least. I was raised for this, just as you," he swatted me lightly on the nose. "Well, just as you don't find the life of a collier despicable. It's just how we live."

"Then why dine with them?" I asked. "Why go through with this?"

"I intend to marry one of them," he said. "Her name is Anya, her father is first cousin to the Czar, and her mother is one of the Greys, one of the old fashionable families of London. She is richer than I shall ever be. She is young now. Too young. But when she is of a more reasonable age, with girlish foolishness behind her, I will ask for her hand, and be given it. She has an allowance that can keep us enjoying our holdings for both of our lives. And her breasts are like melons." He saw my slightly lost look. "Don't look at me like that, mate." He said the word "mate" with a tincture of venom, and it was his way of making fun of my background. It stung. I'd heard it before from the other students who came from money. They were slumming to be in college with those of us who were out of our class. They never let us forget it. "She's pleasant," he continued, "and I very much enjoy being with her. But I don't worry that it's that kind of love that the poets go on about. It's breeding, Justy. She's a virginal heiress with little world experience. She was raised to marry someone like me, and I have spent considerable time ensuring that she will be mine. We're different from you and your people. You have liberties in your daily life, but men like Wendy and I, we have to think about our families and our traditions. There's more to life than just love and chance. There's my great-aunt Minnie to think of, and I support my brother's wife, since he abandoned her. And my father's business needs building. Marriage is not about that passion idea. It's a union that serves the empire, and creates wealth and supports the lower classes as well." He said this all with rehearsed conviction, the way one might overhear someone in church reciting the Nicene Creed.

"Ah," I said, refusing to argue with my jolly companion. "Perhaps I should not drink so much. It may lead me to believe as you."

"Socrates said that bad men live that they may eat and drink, whereas good men eat and drink that they may live. Therefore, we must be good men, for we shall eat and drink to live tonight. But do not worry," he said, coming over to put his hands on my shoulders. He looked at me quite seriously. "We'll abandon the old men and the virgins and go see the whores after dinner."

Chapter Six
How the Rich Eat

1

Dinner was as I expected. The food was a delight, lobster bisque, truffles with pudding, a delicious roast beef and mutton, and fruits of such exotic variety that I thought it had been shipped from Araby.

The wines poured, the brandies sparkled, and I felt fat as a Christmas goose by the end of the meal, and pained from it. The dinner guests were the cause of any indigestion. I spent a stuffy, smothering three hours in which old women spoke of Tennyson and Elizabeth Barrett as if they were radicals, spoke of America as if it would soon become a colony again, and seemed to believe that it was the fashion to flirt in the most obvious ways with much younger men. Most of the young women, inexperienced and full of talk of the latest fashion and musicians and the actors of the London stage, bored me moreso than their elders.

James' young lady, Anya, was different.

2

She sat across the table from me, and at first I didn't glance her way. But when I did, it was her voice that first captured me: an elegant, modulated voice that was not in her head or nasal region, as with the other young women, but deep in her throat, indicating a knowledge of her own body and a certain confidence and serious nature. When I saw her, I held my breath but a moment. An angel of delicacy and purity. She had the porcelain skin so admired in the day, but her cheeks were flushed and red, and she had a bit of sun around her nose and eyes, which I found utterly charming. This was one who did not avoid the noonday sun, nor did she hide from a task. She had the kind of figure in which young men delight, and auburn tresses that fell in what could only be called ringlets around her face, to her shoulders, not pulled back and tightened with ribbons as the others her age had done. Something about her reminded me of my puritanical sister, Bathsheba, who had been a more rustic beauty, but of similar charms. Perhaps it was my sense of purity, of them both. Of the angel. Of the saint. And yet, somewhere lurking beneath the skin, there was the whiff of sensuality, if not decadence (yes, I had felt this even with my sister Bathsheba, and often wondered if she had turned to the local church and hellfire and brimstone because she had felt so drawn to the very pleasures for which she had chastised me.)

Beyond the pleasure of sight and sound, Anya had a nearly aggressive wit, and a direct way of speaking that seemed utterly foreign at the table. Contrary to how James had described her (including his not knowing her precise age), she was an intensely intelligent girl of

The Necromancer

eighteen, who wanted to discuss world politics while her companions offered up bored looks. She was attractive to the eye, and very much the image, to me, of temperate beauty. Her money meant nothing to me, but as I listened to her, and watched her as she spoke, I realized that she was a woman to whom I could attach my affections. And I felt it then, sitting at the table, the biological growl, the animal inside me who sought pleasures of the flesh, as I looked at her. But it wasn't the shape of her breast, or the softness of her powdered skin that made me want to wrap her legs around my hips or press my hand to the back of her head as I held her in a lover's embrace. It was her way of speaking, her interest in France and Germany, in the changes in Mexico, and the news of the abolitionists in America. She was an aware, awake mind, and were she not too young for my interests, I would have, perhaps, invited her for a walk that night to discuss literature and foreign governments. My interest in Anya carried me through the dinner, surrounded by the other dreadful women and men.

The men were not much better, and in some cases, less so, for they spoke of very little except to comment on matters of empire and honor. There was an admiral of the Queen's Navy, and a Scot who was Lord Something of Something, and a young man who was acclaimed as a fine musician who said not a word all night beyond "Please," and "Thank you." James and Wendy were in rare form, pouring libations when the servants hadn't come around fast enough, and chattering with the women, asking the Admiral about wars and campaigns and the sea, and generally fitting in perfectly. I definitely felt that they were out of place at university. It was a bauble for them, or a small medal to add to a collection that they'd keep in a small wooden box on their dressing tables for the rest of their lives. They belonged not among scholars, but in this milieu, as much as did the wallhangings and the pretty birds in their cages in the conservatory. I began to see their money as the doors of a gaol, shutting them in, keeping them safe and away from life itself.

Because I'd buried myself in books and work, I had not been around so many people who were idle in all my life. The phrase kept coming to me, that the devil makes work for idle hands. The Devil's work intrigued me.

I was quizzed from all quarters about the quaint life in a colliery, of what it was like to birth a sheep, although I could not go into much detail for risk of offending one of these silly girls. They treated me as a freak in a show, and in some ways they seemed surprised that a dirty ignorant boy from a distant village, a mongrel in their eyes, could clean up so well, become educated to a moderate degree, and even have friends like James and Wendell. The most annoying questions had to do with my future employment, for as I responded with my plans and interests, I could tell that they thought it such a novelty to have someone at their table who actually had worked in any capacity and would continue to work. There is probably nothing on Earth worse than a class snob from London, and I felt every ounce of the condescension in the room, like it was a lightning bolt that hit me, again and again.

3

At one point, toward the end of dinner, I had to go use the privy (as we often called the outhouse when I had been a boy). In the great mansion in which we had our

The Necromancer

dinner, there were two possibilities for this. In the back alley, behind the house, there was an actual outhouse, made from brick and stone rather than the thrown-together wood of my childhood. But upstairs, there was a room off the bath for this. I chose this latter method of pissing away the wine I'd been drinking, mainly because I wanted to see this elaborate room.

As I went into the bath area, and through it to get to what the owners of the house called a closet, the door was partially open, and I heard someone already using the facility.

I stood outside the little room, but from the slightly open door, I caught a glimpse of the one who used it. It was Anya. I saw a bit of her neck and the curve of her breast. I felt terribly low-class for looking, but I decided to move closer. I had never seen a lady in this position, and if you think me a worm for doing so, so be it. I went to the edge of the doorframe and observed her. She sat astride what seemed a large urn with oriental designs covering it. She had had to lift her gown off in order to use this urn, and her underthings, which were copious, were pulled down and in disarray all around her. Her breasts were held in by a white bodice, laced tight but with the top few stays undone. Her breasts were larger than they'd seemed at the table, and milky white. Her face betrayed no intelligence of my standing near, so I assumed I was safely invisible behind the door. I was both repulsed and attracted as I stood there. I felt arousal, and in the privacy of that moment, was not too disgusted with myself for feeling it.

I imagined opening the door, and throwing her back against the wall, and taking her there, over that enlarged chamber-pot, while she had no defense, neither would she cry out for fear of being ruined.

It was monstrosity within me, this fantasy I had. It was cruel and ruthless and yet provided me with a sense of power and pleasure.

I imagined tearing the bodice from her, ripping out the stays, grinding my face into those virginal breasts while I took her breath away with my thrusts.

And then, as I imagined all this, I drew a quick breath.

Sitting on the urn, she seemed to glance up at me, for a moment.

Had she seen me?

I drew back quickly.

I quietly walked back through the bath area, and nearly bounded down the stairs. I decided to use the privy outside, after all. My heart beat rapidly. Had she seen me watch her? If so, what had she felt? Had she felt terror? Had she been intrigued? Why had I turned to this perversion, this fantasy, while a fine young lady had relieved herself? What disgusting nature had I plumbed within my own flesh?

But when I returned to the table, just in time for the dessert course, she sat there, and engaged me in conversation as if she had not seen or heard a thing. Was this social hypocrisy? Or had she truly not know that a man stood staring at her in her most private of moments, a man who imagined ruining her for the future respectable marriage that her life required? Had she known that someone with the heart of a monster lurked nearby?

The Necromancer

4

Finally, the awful dinner was over. The men retired to the library for cigars and brandy. I was just sober enough to request tea, instead. I sat through the long, endless jokes meant to be considered off-color, but which seemed tame and pointless to me. The men spoke of business dealings, but not directly to me, as I was not then, nor would I ever, be part of their world.

James winked at me, at nearly eleven o'clock, and Wendy tapped his feet impatiently. "We've got a soiree to go to," James whispered to me, glancing at the other men.

"Where are you young gallants off to?" the old admiral asked, cigar smoldering, a slight red line of Madeira on his white mustache.

Wendy quickly said, "The Alfred, I think."

"Or Boodle's," James added, mentioning one of the more famous and distinguished gentlemen's clubs.

"Boodle's? It's popular as ever? I went there as a young man, as well," the old man said.

But when we were out the door, I asked James if this Boodle's or the Alfred were our destinations.

"Those are for the elderly," James said, clapping a hand over my shoulder once we were safely outside, away from the chatter of the social gathering. "We're going to a dangerous place called the Pandemonium. There are some delicious whores I want you to meet."

5

Off in a rush, fresh air and rain greeted us, as the hired cab trotted us down to the third ring of Hell, the despicable, smelly end of the city, through alleys and byways unknown to me. When I looked out into the night, as the cab slowed, I felt foreboding in this area. The streets were crowded with slatterns and urchins, like insects crawling along a feeble light in the darkness. Yet, despite the stink and the crush of humanity, I preferred this—the thing itself, life, the underbelly, the mud beneath the rock—to the soft eiderdown pillow of the rich smothering at my face.

We were all drunk, and I felt apprehensive about following my fellows in through the narrow alleyway, down the cobblestones, heaps of dung just off the main path, to a door that was little more than splintered wood.

"Here you go, Just," Wendy said, stuffing pound notes into my hand. "You'll need this. Do not give me a look about it, take it, it is mine to give and yours to have."

"Dear God," James said, with a sour grimace, "it smells like spume in here. The humanity of it all is stifling."

"And yet," Wendy added, his arm over my shoulder, a bottle of port in his hand. "It is strangely enticing."

"Welcome to the sewer of flesh," James said to me, and pulled me inside the nasty place.

PART TWO
Debauchery

These metaphysics of magicians,
And necromantic books are heavenly!

—Christopher Marlowe, Dr. Faustus

Source of all life, Mother Death,
Plunder me.
Plunder my offering.
Tear the hole of my soul.
Cut me down as I stand in your presence.
—*Justin Gravesend, from the poem/prayer,*
  "Opening the Gate."

Chapter Seven
The Brothel

1

I entered what I thought was like the *cloxa maxima*, the name given to the Roman sewer system of ancient days, for the stench was great, and yet the allure was undeniable.

A large woman, laughing as if life were its own joke, greeted us just inside the door. A cigarillo tipped from the edge of her red lips, she greeted us as the Mother of Harlots that she was, with her bounteous breasts bare, and the stays of her corset open and free, only slightly cupping the monstrous tits, their nipples rouged, one with a small garnet-stone pierced in the aureole. She welcomed my friends, and reached over to hug me, smothering me with the mounds of bosom, which smelled of ginger and sweat. "You're cold, m'dear, but we'll warm you up soon enough."

James and Wendy laughed riotously as they saw me turn blue from lack of breath. "Meet Lady Caroline, Justy," James chortled. "Lady Caroline, you mustn't smother the gentleman!"

When she drew back, she introduced us to the boy-servant she called her helper, "This is Rabbit. Rabbit, I want you to take our guests back into the salon. These are gentlemen, and I expect you should watch how they behave if you wish to move up in this world."

Rabbit, the boy, could not have been more than fourteen, but he looked as if he had aged to sixty—I had heard in my biology studies that there was disease that could do this, and I assumed that keeping the company this unfortunate must needs keep for his work, he might be one of the many bastards born of whores in the city, and the curse of his mother had descended to him, leaving him a child who would die before he was a man. His skin was wrinkled, and his eyes, sunken, as if he had never been truly young in all his life.

I soon learned the reason for his nickname, for he hopped about as he went, and I began to see him less as an unfortunate, and more as someone who had found the world in which he might thrive, despite the vagaries of an indifferent Deity.

2

We followed hopping Rabbit through this house of ill repute, its maze-like rooms decorated with imitation frescos of satyrs with enormous penises jabbing helpless nymphs and dryads, as well as wall murals that seemed from India, of turbaned and silk-clothed rajahs with engorged members tipped like red arrows pressing into

The Necromancer

the yielding caverns of veiled women who kissed and pinched each others' breasts. The colors in the flickering wall lamps were muted browns and yellows and reds. In the wide rooms off the hall, gentlemen with their trousers unbuttoned and their blousy shirts thrown open, their collars hanging at their shoulders, grasped the available female flesh—the wenches and unfortunates whose chief talent involved their tongues and their hips, and it struck me, as it had before, how pleasure for one was rarely pleasure for another. Surely these slatterns and strumpets could not enjoy this work, this labor, anymore than I enjoyed my early work in the colliery, among the spoil heaps and caverns. But the gentlemen did not mind, for they were lost in their own ecstasies, as they squeezed and rammed and tasted. Walking down the hallway, poorly lit by mutton-candle sconces, I heard the moans and slurpings of human lust. In the flickering candlelight, I saw the forms against the wall, men pressed against women, men against men, but all in shadow, all not quite seen, and a strange slowness to their movements as if they were snake charmers, careful not to make a wrong move for fear of getting bitten. Because of the brandy I'd consumed that night, I couldn't quite focus on these actors of the libido, and we pushed past them to another doorway, and through this door, we came to a large room—a salon, filled with overstuffed lounges and a bar at one end. Here, it was a bit more dignified, although the décor and the mode of dress left no question about what the business of the house might be. The walls had paintings of naked women, their legs lazily spread, or classical themes of Bacchus, engorged, chasing a wood nymph, and a few of Leda and the Swan by various artists of lessening talents.

"Sir," Rabbit said, cupping his small hands together.

James whispered in my ear, "Generosity to the poor, mate."

I reached into my pocket, and withdrew fourpence.

Rabbit's eyes lit up when he saw what landed in his hands.

"I say," Wendy said. "Don't give too much. You'll ruin these people. The whores are no more than three quid, if that."

"Two for five," James added, gleefully.

In the salon, the women were bare-breasted like the proprietress, and walked around, amazons on the hunt, carrying pints and pitchers of bitter and ale. The men sat, talking with each other, laughing at jokes, or playing cards at one of several low tables set up. In some respects, it was a more democratic society than the dinner party I'd just left, for women smoked and dealt cards, and I overheard one conversation where one of the whores spoke about news of the famine in Ireland. The men were of the upper classes, all, dressed as if for a fancy dress ball, and looking as wealthy rakes might when relaxed: as if the need for relief and release is tantamount to reaching heaven itself.

Rabbit hopped off to get me a beer, but I had one, from a mustachioed whore, faster than he could retrieve a drink. When he returned, I took the pint from him, and set it down. "Here," I said, offering another tuppence. "For your trouble."

"Thankee, sir."

"Rabbit, can you tell me something?"

"Sir?"

"Why is this place called the Pandemonium?"

"It is because it is, sir."

"Pandemonium is a peculiar name," I said. "It implies the Devil."

"The master," he said, an impish look to his aged face.

"The master?"

"The one what owns it." Then, in a broken Cockney, Rabbit told me of the man who, sitting in a corner of the salon, was the richest man in all the world, richer than the Queen, and he had his wealth because he sold his soul to the Devil. "We all knows it," Rabbit said. "But we likes bein' 'ere, and we don't mind the Dewiwl so long's the marks come in reg'lar."

I paid Rabbit a one pound note, and he nearly kissed my hand over it, and went hopping off, happy that he'd earned in a moment more than he probably had in the past month or more.

Then, I turned back to watch this so-called "master."

3

He was not like the others. Yes, he had an air of the aristocrat about him. He held his cane and gloves just so, and his hair was cut in the current fashion, and he had the long unremarkable face of the city gentleman.

But he was more alive in his eyes than everyone else sitting in that salon.

He wasn't there for a girl.

He was there for all of it. A whoremaster? Hardly. This man looked as if he could, indeed, sell his soul to the Devil.

And the Devil would want it.

I immediately wanted to meet him. James was stunned that I was not ready to grab a wench and take off for one of the private rooms upstairs. "Take two or three," he said as he pressed coins into my hand. "These girls will let you do anything you like." Then, he said something that only struck me as odd later, as the night wore on. He winked and said, "All right, then, mate, you shall find us when you need us. But you must try the whores here. They're fabulous creatures."

But I had no interest. If I wanted sex, I had my life for it. But I wanted to meet the man whose dark eyes seemed to know something more about the world than I could learn on my own.

4

I have learned since that his ability had to do with what is called "the glamour," and that is a level of connectedness to the world that one only gets when under the influence of a particular narcotic, Lotos (not "Lotus," but certainly meant in the same spirit as the classical lotus of Homer's poem), in the parlance of the sect that harvests its nectar and administers it to those willing to risk using it, in small doses. But then, I just knew that he was magnetic, and I wanted to know something of what he knew.

Without even being sure how I moved so swiftly to him, I stood before him, offering my hand. "Sir," I bowed, slightly, feeling as if he were some prince of the realm.

He waved me off, a dismissive gesture with his hands. "I'm busy," he said.

"May I...may I sit here." I indicated the seat beside him.

"If you wish," he said.

"I am Justin."

He nodded, but said nothing. He kept staring at the others. I looked among them, and saw my friend Wendy grab a girl's breast, stroking it lightly. Then, they went off through a second door, presumably to the upstairs rooms.

"All of them," the man said, "animals." I would like to say that this distinguished looking gentleman had an equally distinguished voice, but in fact, he had a slightly cockney accent, but with an upper crust twist. "Look at them. Feeding on each other. Bloodsuckers. Wasting their energies."

"You own this establishment?"

"You're from the country."

"Yes, sir," I said. "Manchester."

"No, I mean the country. Wales?"

I nodded. "The North-East part."

"A collier."

"I was, sir."

"Are you the one I was brought here to meet?"

"Sir?"

"I was brought here tonight to meet someone tonight," he said. "I was called."

"Sir, it was not me. I only arrived in London today, and am staying with friends."

"Ah," he said. "Your friends are here. They bring you to London to see this. The carnival. The flesh pit."

"No, sir. They brought me here to enjoy a few days respite from studies."

"A student? I should've guessed. You are a poor boy who has clawed his way, using his talents, using whatever is at his disposal, to rise in the world. But this world, this world you see, has no interest in your concerns. Tell me, boy, why aren't you coupling with one of these ladies? Why aren't you in the hall, or upstairs on a sodden mattress, your cannon roaring? Isn't this the sport you students enjoy so much?"

"I don't find this interesting," I said. "And I'm not a boy."

"Of course you're not, not like our little friend, Rabbit" he said. He reached over, and pressed his finger just under my chin. He felt my pulse. I could feel my heart beat beneath his cold finger. I felt wicked for thinking it, but when he touched me, I experienced a strange and lewd excitement, as if he were forcing some intimacy upon me that both felt good but also felt wrong. As he leaned into the lamplight, I gasped. His face was a smooth alabaster — like a statue, white and cold, and yet handsome in a smooth, unnerving way. His lips seemed to have the pinkness of youth, and his nose, aquiline and noble. Only his eyes, in the flickering light, put fear into me, for the pupils were dilated, engorged and blackened. I will admit that I had only seen this on one human being before:

A corpse.

In my brief study of medicine, I had gotten close to a corpse after examination, and its open eyes were like this. When I asked why, the surgeon told me that it had to do with the trauma that had caused the man's death as well as some unusual chemical poured into the eye after death. It made the eye look as if it were a large shiny black marble.

"You are twenty. Your name is Justin. Justin Grave. Graverson." Then, he let go. He smiled, slightly. "You

The Necromancer

are him who I was meant to meet here. You are my reason for haunting this place. Shall I tell you something about yourself, Justin? Shall I? Shall I tell you that I know your soul, and that you have given yourself to pleasures and to death, and you long for something that cannot be held in our world, but only in the next?"

I listened to him with a sense of dislocation. He seemed familiar to me now, as if he were my father, but the kind father I had not yet met. He seemed someone to whom I wanted to be near, to touch in some way. My arousal for the whores (for it would be ridiculous for me to deny that the sight of the nearly naked women, their bosoms rising and falling as they laughed in the arms of men who stroked them, would not bring me to full goathood—my phallus straining against my trousers—as the whole world now seemed a flesh carnival made only for my enjoyment) had heated my skin, and flooded my mind with visions and a long-forgotten taste of a woman's swampy venus delta.

And the man who sat with me now, speaking in sonorous tones, with the eerily pale skin and eyes like stone, seemed part of the arousal itself.

"You were born to what you are about to receive, my boy. You were meant for this, for my world, for the future."

I sighed when he spoke, no doubt like a girl in love, because all my life I had wanted to be destined for something greater than where I had been born. All my life, I had felt that missing thing, that half of me, my twin, my other, the one who knew of me and yet had not reached me.

And this man, much older than myself, and yet still young and virile and masterful, might be that one. I write here not of a sexual nature, but of a compelling magnetism that I could not resist, nor would I, even if given the choice.

"I am your Master," he said. "I am he who is meant to initiate you into the truth of who you are."

In that moment, I believed him, and accepted the adventure he offered.

Then, he took his gloves up, and rose. "Come with me, Justin. I want to show you something. Something extraordinary."

Chapter Eight
The Three Rooms

1

The smells of the rooms were intensely conflicted: perfumes the likes of which had not scented harems outside of Araby, mingled with the stench of human sweat and sexual congress. If one believes that fornication is pleasure, one only need dispute this when smelling its effects with many fornicators doing what they love the most. It is the human body at its most pained. And yet, its most pleasured. We watch the act of fertility with disdain. It brings us to the level of dogs. And yet, within each act, if we are the participant, the excitement and feelings make us believe we are entering the pure realm of godhood. So the participants in these rooms, and in the recesses of the corridors, must have felt their urgent mission of lust to be uplifting; afterward, looking at their compatriots, they surely must've been struck by the futility and the filth of life itself, and the source of life, the act of the phallus invading the opening of another, which then engulfed and devoured the manhood. And this is what I observed with my guide pointing out the more lewd and twisted body formations around us.

I followed him like a puppy in need of a master, through several rooms, passing by mattresses and writhing bodies. "There are three rooms I want you to see tonight. You will observe those things that you may find most repulsive, perhaps," he said. "Does that frighten you?"

"No," I said, and meant it, for I developed a keen curiosity about him and this place. Truth be told, I had dreams that were much more lurid than even the heaving bodies that slammed and pressed each other in the dank corners of this brothel. Nor, I admit, was I a stranger to the whore, for in Manchester, with friends, I had visited them once or twice, although in circumstances much less elaborate than the Pandemonium.

He led me first into one large room, upon which was a sumptuous bed. The room was well-lighted, and in one corner, an African serving girl, coifed in the older style of powdered wig and a ladies' riding suit, played the clavier near the entrance, a lively tune with an unusual rhythm. When I entered the room, she alone turned to look at me, and I discovered that it was not a girl at all, but a young man dressed as a girl.

2

I passed this musician, and stepped in further, for it seemed there was a small crowd therein. Over the bed, a great mirror. Beside the bed, two manservants, wearing only trousers, sat, holding long, intricately-carved pipes that released a thin, lazily swirling smoke. These were opium pipes. Around the bed, sat several well-dressed young ladies and older men, stout and puffy of face. A peculiar sweet smell was in the air, mixed with something like wormwood. The audience looked as if they were meant to be at the opera. Instead, they watched the spectacle on the bed.

The servants' masters were in the bed, pleasuring a wench sandwiched between them, their shirts only half torn from their bodies. Buttocks thrust before and behind. I was repulsed by this public display moreso than the other rooms, for there was a strange refinement to it, and it seemed less about the pleasure and more about the spectacle. And yet, I, like the other spectators, wanted to watch. The moans of lust became loud, and seemed like chants to me, and then, in the mirror above, I saw the faces of the participants, and recoiled.

My schoolchums, James and Wendy, pressed into the whore, their hair flying, their eyes rolled up so much into their sockets that all I saw was whiteness, and worse than my friends taking their carnal pleasures, the woman in between them was none other than the angel of purity I had seen at the dinner party:

Anya, the one whom James intended to marry.

The lady I had spied upon in her private moments.

It looked—if this scene were to be believed—as if my friends were taking their liberties with her just as I had dreamed of doing.

Surely, I thought, this was a charade for my benefit, this was a whore who had been made up to look like that most chaste young maiden. Surely this could not be the virgin who at the dinner table was fascinating with art and politics and seemed so much finer than her dinner companions, whose milk-white breasts had invitingly been displayed for me, briefly, without her knowledge.

Behind me, I heard my guide's voice, "Do you see the beauty of it? And do you see the monstrosity?"

I nodded. With much sadness, I said, "Is this the extraordinary thing you wanted me to witness? The debauchery of an innocent at the hands of two libertines?"

"No, my friend. The extraordinary is yet to come. This is the world, and it is no better than this bedroom," he said. "Most human beings watch those with power take their pleasures from the innocent and unknowing. She is drugged, you see. She is innocence. They are all guilty, not just the two men, but those who watch and smile. The world is full of spectators, watching the debauchery of others. Watching and applauding its corruption. Look at them, with their fascination at seeing this event. Who in the world is not like this, willing to sit in judgment in the bedroom of others, to clap and hoot and live only through the eyes and not through the soul, and enjoy the humiliation of innocence? The lady in question does not even know she is here. She is dreaming, perhaps. She is not aware of her surroundings. Tomorrow, she shall awaken in her bed, not sure what has happened, seeing of these same men and women in her daily life, not being certain if she experienced a nightmare or if, in fact, she has merely been a puppet in their despicable fantasy." Then, he touched my shoulder. "But come, Justin. There is more to see here."

I went with him, drunk, not understanding, not knowing if this were all a lie, a show, if Anya hadn't been

The Necromancer

at the dinner that night, a whore dressed up as a lady, or if she were a lady, drugged, kidnapped and brought into this den of depravity by my two rakish chums who, in my mind, seemed common criminals for this terrible show. Confusion took over my mind, and I could not believe that James and Wendy were the sorts to do this to a young lady, nor would I believe that Anya was a whore who pretended to society. I began to wonder if something of the poppy had not been slipped into my own drinks that night.

And yet, I went with the owner of the Pandemonium, out into the corridor, and down a dimly lit hallway.

3

Into the next room we went, and this one was much smaller than the one previous. Here, there was nothing, nor was there anyone but a small figure, cloaked in some sort of black cape, bent down in the far corner of the room.

"Go to," he said.

I went over to the figure, and saw that it was not a person at all, but a carved stone statue of a saint, in an aspect of prayer.

I turned to my guide, wondering.

"This is God," he said.

"This is not God."

"He is in this room, and this is His miracle. A stone image of His work. The image of man. In the image of God. Do you feel Him? Smell Him? Can He be in this room in a house among whores and thieves and drunkards?"

"They say that He can be anywhere."

"Then, He is here. This is his room. But where are his worshippers? They are elsewhere, they surround him in other rooms, obeying the laws of the flesh rather than His laws."

"Why do you show me this?"

"It is to show you that even in the midst of the worst of humanity," the gentleman said, "God does nothing. God cares little. Only this statue sits, bent at prayer, hoping to become something other than stone."

I laughed, enjoying the joke, feeling somehow less disturbed. So, this was a carnival, a play, a show for me to enjoy. I wondered if all new visitors to the Pandemonium were treated to this grand tour. I thought of my father, and how he would've cried out to Heaven to save himself from such heathen and godless behavior, and it made me warm to think that I had ended up at the same place he would've considered a vision of Hell.

I left the strange little room and its odd statue, and followed him down the last several feet of the corridor.

4

The hall ended abruptly.

"What of the last room? The third?" I asked.

The gentleman then produced a key from his waistcoat, and proceeded to open a door that I would not have noticed had he not known where to turn the key. The door, smaller than most, opened on a long staircase downward. I had to crouch down to fit through the door, as did he. There were lamps lit along the wooden stairs, and again, I followed him, this time into the bowels of the building.

The Necromancer

When we reached the bottom step, it seemed darker there, and I hestitated before taking another step forward.

Gently, he took my hand. In the shadows, I could barely see his face. "You must come, Justin. This is why we had to meet. This is what drew me here tonight, and you."

He led me through the shadow of this underground lair, and soon enough we came to another door, behind which were voices.

"Where are we going?" I asked.

"To speak with the Dead," he said.

Visionary 3

Now, I can see them better—there are four of them, coming from the burning forest, loping toward me with their teeth showing yellow and sharp, and the puffed skin around their eyes, their many eyes, red and wounded, and I continue to batter at the door to keep it open, to keep the portal wide. I hear the moans of my chosen one, but I continue to tear at him, to scrape my fingers across his flesh, as the creatures—the gods—come to me, their arms raised in joy and hunger, their nethermouths opening, revealing shiny black teeth beneath the folds of their bellies.

Tentacles of pleasure shoot from me, like light from pinholes in a shadowbox, I AM BECOMING! I AM TRANSFORMING FROM MY FLESH OUTWARD! My subject, beneath me, held and clawed by me, feels the tendrils of my energy pressing along his flesh, into the soft lubricity of his skin, which is shimmering like a lake, and rippling as if hundreds of pebbles are being thrown into it, but not pebbles, my tentacles, my slim quivers, my quills, thrust into his back and thighs, along his shoulders, into his neck, curving around to enter the holes of his ears, and, like a starfish opening a clam, they reach around to his mouth, to his clenched teeth, and pry him open there, to enter him, to take the sacrifice offered, to possess him completely.

The burning within the pathways of my body is heaven itself, is a feeling of well-being and weightlessness, and I begin to possess him, to tear him, to gnaw at him, and the gods approach, and reach for his eyes.

Chapter Nine
The Room of Sighs

1

I laughed when we entered the large, well-appointed room. I knew now I must have been drugged in my cups, for I felt wonderful and light, and resisted nothing.

Like the upstairs rooms, it was lit with cheap candles secured onto the walls, and a mural of debauchery encircled all within the room. But these debaucheries seemed less innocent than those in the front hallways of the Pandemonium. The paintings were of knights, in full black armor, their codpieces arched and made to look very much like their lances, their gauntlet-covered hands pressing deep into the openings of a young lass, one at her mouth, one at each ear, and the greatest knight of all, his hand over her maidenhead. There was nothing pleasurable about the image, nor did it incite my imagination, for there was something wholly disgusting about the knights and their defenseless victim, whose naked body was painted with symbols of an occult nature. Then, in another part of the mural, a man was tied to a cross that was shaped like an X, and two women stood near him with small knives, having just made incisions along his spinal column. They were flaying him alive, and the look on the young man's face, who underwent this torture, was one of a martyred saint experiencing ecstasy, while his torturers wore expressions of beatific grace. Along another wall, men copulated with fantastic beasts, including gorgons and harpies and unicorns and gryphons. In one panel, a gryphon held a man down with its talons and took him from behind, an enormous and scaled phallus pressed into the curves of the man's buttocks; in another, a unicorn's horn pressed into the folds of a woman's innards while a man, standing over her, pressed a small dagger into his own belly, a full erection beneath this. Other creatures populated the mural, including beautiful women whose faces had been obliterated into whiteness, whose nipples had become open mouths with rows upon rows of teeth, and whose netherparts were as those of baboons, the female organ large and red and engorged, or men with the heads of fish, five arms, all clutching some otherworldly vine from which grew a small blue flower, their arms ending in tentacles and small whips of hair. It was wondrous and terrible. The images were nightmarish, and yet strangely beautiful, but did not match the spectacle within the room itself.

2

Writhing on the floor, an orgy of flesh.

It was not the Dead who were there, but several young

men and women, all quite beautiful and well-groomed, and they fondled each other on several mattresses. On straw mats in a corner, men lay down on pillows while young women offered them the opium pipe. Some seemed to have an aristocratic bearing, the shiny hair of the rich, the clean, well oiled skin, the slender, the athletic. Others less so, darker, with a Celtic look to them, smaller, and yet no less appetizing to consider as they rutted and rolled. It was yet another level of the brothel, and I was a little relieved when I realized that this was yet another metaphorical Hell, as the first two rooms he had shown me had been of Social Hypocrisy, I assumed, and then of the Silence of God. This must be The Sins of the Flesh, and it was a good deal merrier and more alluring that the other rooms.

"Do you like them?" my guide asked, pointing out two women frolicking on some pillows, tenderly kissing each other, and patting each other's buttocks. Isolated from the outside world like this, truly, I felt my animal nature take over, and that growling beast came out.

"Yes," I replied, or perhaps only thought I replied. My breathing slowed as if the very air I needed were being denied me. I felt my body moreso than my mind.

"Go on," he said. "They're yours. Go to them."

In other circumstances, I might've run from that room, but I was still a young man, and my libido had been aroused by the entire venture into this playground of the Devil. Furthermore, there was something of the somnambulist about this man. I felt as if I were in his power, or else I had given my will over to him for this adventure. I imagined this was the feeling of Adam, taking the apple to his lips, knowing that it was forbidden, and terrible, understanding that there would be consequences and attacks of conscience on the morrow. But the allure and the opportunity. I had nothing drawing me back. No woman, no obligation, no sense that this would even be known outside this room.

My member was hard and whatever power Nature has over any one of us, She had over me at that moment more powerfully than I had ever before felt it. I felt that I would die right then if I didn't find a warm harbor in the hips of those women, that I needed the acceptance of the naked human flesh, the sea of rapture awaited.

3

I waded through the writhing bodies—the two men who caressed a woman who arched her back and pressed both sides of herself into their lower regions. On a mattress, a young man with a long member thrust himself quickly and with accompanying groans, into a woman with wide, inviting hips. Two men lay together, stroking each other, while a woman kissed each of them passionately on the lips. I felt a strange, compelling want, a hunger, to let go of any restraint within my mind. I was in London, and moreover, I was in an underground chamber of sin, lust, and pleasure. Further, I was somehow within the grasp of my puppeteer-host, and felt as if I were meant to perform in this play, before him. My mind seemed to turn off to some degree, for this kind of sexual play appealed to the libido and not the conscious mind. It all seemed as if it were permissive, allowed, and I went to the two soft women, and pressed myself against them, between them. My fine clothes peeled away, layer by layer, my neck held and rubbed and kissed. They

The Necromancer

licked me and caressed me, both of their mouths going to my privates, their bodies turned around, and I tasted them and smelled their essence, and it was as if I had smoked the opium myself, for I felt my mind somehow dissolve, like the rain outside, and my mind was no longer located beneath my scalp, but was in my pores, in my fingers, along my thighs, in my toes — as if every part of my being were thinking by way of touching.

Others joined us. I felt foggy and distant, although the impulses in my skin seemed to grow. Every touch was an awakening to something new. I felt the rough touch of a young man my own age as he grasped me around the waist. I did not register revulsion, nor did I wish him not to hold me thus. And the women, my hands between their thighs, a whisper of obscenity in my ear, someone taking each of my toes in her mouth and holding it as if it were a rare dessert. I have never felt such delight in perversion as I did then, and if part of me felt this were wrong, if my religious upbringing had any warning bell going off, I somehow let it ring without responding to it. The pleasure, again. The pleasures of carnality were upon me, and I was a reveler. I rolled in this garden of ecstasy, feeling caresses and thrusts and mouths and warmth and wetness, all the while my mind seemed to turn as black as the skies over my home village, a seeping darkness that betokened nothing, while my sensory organs flickered and sputtered with a sense of being extinguished and awakened, over and over again.

I forgot my guide, my host, the mysterious gentleman, until the banquet of sensual delights was devoured.

Then, awakening from the slow withdrawal from pleasure and flesh, that terrible cracked feeling as if one is broken and now needs mending, I saw him standing over me. He had been watching.

I felt naked and ashamed, and reached for my shirt. I became aware of the filthiness of the act, of the uncouth nature of my own body and its compulsions. As I wrapped my shirt about my shoulders, I noticed the others.

I tell you, I saw the most terrifying thing that could be seen at that moment.

Not the beautiful men and women of this paradisical brothel, this private room within the rooms.

But corpses.

I knew a corpse well enough from the laboratory, from the medical amphitheater in Manchester.

The skin, the signs of putrefaction, the slightly bloated nature, the eyes, the way the musculature had changed owing to the lack of that spark of life.

They lay around me, and I could identify each one. The buttocks of the beautiful man with the gentle lips. The twin, slightly lopsided breasts of the young lady with the curled hair, her ribbons falling around her Botticelli face and shoulders. The two dark haired men pressed, still, so close to their lovely companion, her mouth still gaping in a parody of orgasmic joy. Or, perhaps, a scream.

Those I had only just left off embracing.

The women and the men, naked, and beautiful, and so dead that their skin was of a bluish hue, and their eyes, staring at nothing, as if they'd only just come from the arms of Mother Death.

The Necromancer

4

"Did you love them?" he asked.

I sat shivering, unsure of my surroundings, unsure if I had been drugged or somehow tricked and these were not lifeless beings but dolls, or actors playing tricks.

"The Dead can love," he continued. "They are here, all the time. They speak to us, but we do not hear them. And we can speak to them."

"Who are you?" I asked, feeling as if I had just crawled into a room in my mind that I might never open again. Trying to make sense of this night before insanity took hold, before the disease of what I had done grasped my heart.

"I am your master," he said. "And was called by one who is Dead to find you."

Then, he held something up before me. I did not recognize it at first.

"I raised him up and spoke to him, and he brought me the secrets of the other realm," he said. And then, from his bundle, he produced the small skull, cleaned of grit and hair and filth. "He brought you and I together. You will wake tomorrow, this will be a dream, but if your soul finds no rest, you will find me again. You will find the one you have sought your whole life."

At the back of the skull, the part of it that had been smashed in by some small knife or other tool.

My brother's bones.

Chapter Ten
The Seeker

1

Then, the smell of pine and sweet treacle in my nose, a gaseous mixture of some sort, I blacked out.

2

I awoke to a strange rumbling, my head pounding. I had been drugged, I thought, and somehow my dream of orgy and its stygian aftermath was simply induced by opium, or perhaps the brandy mixed with some foreign liqueur. Brothels were notorious for this kind of thing, and I could not have expected anything less from a house of ill repute called the Pandemonium.

When I opened my eyes, the sunlight itself seemed like hammers pounding at me. I lay in the bed to which I must have been ushered earlier in the day while passed out—at the house at Regent's Park, owned by my chum, James. I tried to retrace my last memories of the night. All

I could recall was the terrible scene of horror, surrounded by the beautiful bodies of the dead, and the feeling that I had been fondling, holding, licking, and even physically entering them. I knew of stories of necrophiliacs, those who enjoyed copulation with corpses, and I shuddered to think of what I might have done. Or dreamed. I felt waves of revulsion go through me. I lay a long time, clutching my pillow and bedclothes, looking up at the ceiling of my room, trying to understand how I could've had such a dream, or such a strong feeling that it had not been a dream at all.

Yet, surely, I argued within myself, you've had nights of drunken wanderings in which you imagined things done that may not have been done. Or done things without knowing you had done them, later. Surely, this had been such a night. How many brandies had been drunk before dinner? How much wine with dinner? And the port afterward? And the madeira? The pint of ale at the brothel, surely I had at least one while there? How could I possibly have experienced the feeling of those women touching me, urging me into their bodies, and how could I have allowed a man to grasp me about the waist without fighting him? Surely this was a dream that meant I should not drink so much in one night!

After several minutes of convincing myself of the impossibility of the previous night's revel, I rose, trembling from the effects of too much alcohol, and stumbled and fumbled my way to the chamber pot in the well-appointed bath down the hall.

The Necromancer

3

The day was a normal one. James and Wendy, too, were suffering the effects of the previous night. When we sat in a parlor, speaking of school and sports, I could not get the images of them out of my head, of their ecstasy and grimace, their groans of animal conquest as they plundered the angel of virtue, fair Anya. Yet, I had the distinct impression that they were none the worse, whether it had happened or not. And to be sure, I became convinced by the minute that it could not have happened, for they certainly would be mentioning it now, or alluding to it in some way. To provoke this, I brought up Anya's name, mentioning her beauty, and James laughed and told me that she was not nearly as beautiful as the whores had been the previous night.

"Do you remember who you bedded?" I asked.

"The sordid details, mate?" James laughed, heartily, and then groaned because even his laugh caused him distress, he was suffering so from the effects of drink. "I took two for my fun, and they were lovely girls, but this is not a subject for discussion." Here, his voice quieted, because of the nearby servants. "Suffice it to say, it was sweet and over too fast."

"And you?" I asked my other friend.

"I don't talk of this stuff," Wendy said. "Say, shall we go to the opera tonight?"

"Opera bores me," James said. "What about the Blackfriars?"

"Wonderful," Wendy said. He turned to me, "The Blackfriars Club is a sporting place. You will love it, Justin."

They continued their conversation, turning toward

horses and their plans for the next few days, but my mind was elsewhere. The three rooms, the orgy, all of it had seemed so real, but it was as if it were a truth of night, whereas daylight brought a different truth.

I had the unsettling feeling as the day wore on that there was truth to my memory, or at least a beveled truth, bending the last of my memory round the curved edges of my sense of reality.

I began to remember further details of the night, and took leave of my companions and set off for a walk through the gardens of the Park, just off the Square. It was a gorgeous late spring afternoon, and the Park was empty save for ladies walking in groups or nursemaids with their charges at the benches, feeding ducks or buying sugar candy from the vendors. As I watched them, I began to feel what I can only describe as deviant urges. I observed the young ladies, and wished to, in that perfect day, grab them, and tear their fineries from them, exposing their white flesh to the burning sun, and taking them right there, in front of the matrons and the nursemaids. Taking them, like some human monster, and enjoying their cries and whimpers. It was a terrible self-loathing that then came over me, that I could watch these decent ladies and imagine pummeling them from mouth to fundament, and savoring their degradation. It was disgusting, and I set off from the park, profoundly disturbed by my dream from the previous night, and from my monstrous thoughts along the garden path.

I knew I was not a monster, and yet I found myself uncomfortable in my own skin.

The Necromancer

4

A man may walk many miles in a few hours if he feels the Devil at his heel.

I wandered the city, thinking I might need a church, although I tended to avoid them. Yet, my upbringing, between my puritanical father and devoutly Catholic mother, could not be denied. I felt better in church, and felt I needed to go there to somehow purge myself of these unnatural feelings. I found a church on Gower Street, and entered straight away. It was empty, and cold, but the large crucifix at the front, by the altar, and the windows that depicted the saints and martyrs, brought me some comfort. I went and sat down, and prayed a bit, or tried. But my mind kept returning to sexual force and power, and a feeling of wanting to go into the streets and grab the first man or woman there, and to lick a human ear while tearing at the fabric of trousers, or ripping the bodice from an unsuspecting and chaste maiden. I sat, aroused in God's house, and when I looked at the stained glass of the windows, I didn't see St. Francis praying with animals, but saw him, his monk's robes up around his waist, his enormous phallus rammed into the haunches of a donkey...or St. George, his lance going into not a dragon, but a crouching woman, her buttocks splayed and her pudenda bright pink...of a saint I could not identify, a woman martyr, perhaps, her fingers pressed into her quim, plucking at it...

And then I looked up at the cross, it was not Jesus I saw there, but my own father, and beneath him, my older sister Bathsheba, pleasuring him with her tongue. I am cursed! I railed within myself. Blasphemy comes out of my mind! Malicious pictures plague my thoughts!

What drug had been given me the previous night? I wondered. What madness and degeneracy had befallen me that I should see these visions? I covered my eyes, and then bit down hard on my lower lip, drawing blood, just to feel something, to know that I was real, and these mad thoughts and dreams were merely the result of poisoning of some sort.

When I opened my eyes, the church and its figures and windows had returned to their former sacred states.

I felt a sense of panic, as if God watched me now, in His house, watched and judged me, and worse, there was no forgiveness in this sense. I felt the thudding of my own heart in my chest, and wondered if this were what one felt just before death. I went out into the streets, which seemed desolate and unwelcoming. I ran down side streets as one afraid that the Devil himself might be chasing me, were I to look back. Any stranger I saw seemed threatening, and I dared not look at women or men, for fear that I would inflict some diabolical act upon them.

I arrived at a public house, and went in, thirsty and feverish. I bought several pints, and managed to drown some of my fear. The palpitations in my breast lessened.

I was surrounded by men very much like those from my home village—workmen from Scotland and Wales and the boroughs surrounding the city, tarred nearly black with pitch or coal dust, or covered with the white powder of plastering and bricklaying work. I felt a sense of calm.

After an hour or so, I went out into the twilight, the first of the gas lamps being lit. The street narrowed, and I had a choice of going right onto a wide avenue, or to

The Necromancer

the left, into an side street with a shambles of lower class apartments above steamy laundries and other vice houses. Although my conscious mind bid me go to the open boulevard, my body yearned for something in that darkening street, and as I walked, and walked some more, I realized that I had come, at last, to the alley in which stood the place called the Pandemonium.

I knew I had to enter it again.

5

When I crossed its threshold, I was taken aback.

It was empty.

Not empty as if it would later fill, as the midnight hour approached.

But empty as if it had never been full at all.

There were no signs in the corridor of the perverted couplings of men and women, nor of the carnival shouts of the fat, boisterous madam and her small assistant, Rabbit, who hopped along after her. It looked as if it had been abandoned for several days. I went room to room, remembering the shadow figures of heat and flesh, as Rabbit hopped ahead of me, taking me down the hall to the main salon. The murals remained on the walls, with their lewd figures and exotic positions. But it looked as if the place had not been occupied for months.

The door to the salon was missing, and as I stepped through the doorway, I saw that the place had been blackened by some kind of fire. The lamps were aglow, however, which meant that someone was there, someone still kept the lights going. Then, I followed my memory trail into another hall, the way that the Master had taken me, but when I came to the place where the keyhole in the wall had been, there was nothing. Just wall. No door. No keyhole.

A dead end.

And then, someone grabbed me from behind, so swiftly that I got the wind knocked out of me. I held onto consciousness, and tried to fight my attacker with all I had.

Something soft—a kerchief?—went to my mouth, and it smelled like treacle and tar, that same sweet stink I'd smelled the previous night, and no matter how I fought, I felt myself grow weaker. It was not the smell of the sort of ether used in the medical laboratory, but it seemed to possess similar properties.

I awoke, possibly a few minutes later, in restraints, tied to a bed. I tugged at the strips of leather that held me at my wrists and ankles. Over my mouth, a tight cloth to keep me from speaking. I felt utterly powerless and vulnerable.

A voice in the shadowy darkness, the Master of the previous evening, "You have been the one sent to us, you have passed the first test of our Order, and now the most arduous of tests shall press you to the limit of your mind. Yes, against your will. For your will must be broken."

6

I cannot write here of the degradations that befell me in the dark pit of Hell. I close my mind to its memory. To the prodding, and the pleasure that was terror, and what grasped me, and what gave itself to me, but it was all human, and all flesh, and of many types and aspects, a deviant, depraved sort of rape of my body and my will.

I fought against it, and yet, in my mind, my brother's bones were foremost.

How had this Master gotten them? What had they to do with me here?

I will say that at the end of the hours of pleasure and agony, I prayed for Death.

I prayed to join my brother.

Yet the worst came, after.

A large, muscular man who looked as if he were a hired murderer, came with two assistants whose faces had been painted egg-shell white, and began pressing needles into my flesh, slowly, methodically. I had no strength to fight, and I was afraid of their needles. They worked for many hours, tattooing images onto my back and buttocks and thighs, across my belly and chest, as well. When they were done, they drew out small tools—as if they were stone carvers. I tried to scream, but found that my throat was unable to emit more than a bleat. They had jewels and rings, and I felt the first pain in my left nipple as a long sharp needle went into it. Then, a small ruby was attached, as a gypsy might wear a jewel in his ear. Other parts of my body were thus beringed and bejeweled, and the horrors of it were minor in the plan of all things, but when I lay there, feeling the fire of needles and the cold touch of the rings as they pierced my genitals, and my tongue, and at the arc of my navel, I felt as if each press down into my flesh would be the one that would kill me. The pain was excruciating, and waves of unconsciousness befell me, although I awoke, blearily, through the worst of it, wanting to cry out in pain.

7

When it was over, I felt a warm hand untie me. Bare-breasted young women washed me with sponges, and anointed oils and perfumes on my skin and in my scalp. The tattoos were rubbed and gently dressed. Any wounds or cuts I had (for the small knives had sliced bits of my flesh beneath my arms, and near my thigh during a profoundly horrible hour) were taken care of, and a salve of some kind was rubbed into the reddened areas where my body had been pierced with jewels and small golden rings and round studs. My hair was trimmed, and my nails were buffed. I was clothed in a blouse that seemed to be made of gold, and in trousers that were thin and dark. Boots were brought, and slender maidens with veils over their faces pressed my feet into them. I was given water, which I drank greedily, and allowed a place to eliminate wastes, all the while my hands were not free, but held firmly. The degredations were continual, and yet there was a beauty to them. I felt like a child, just being born.

It was my rebirth.

Thus, dressed, and cared for, I slept again until someone came and woke me.

8

When I awoke, I was in a very different place. It was a hall of sorts, not unlike the medical amphitheater in Manchester, where I watched corpses being dissected. I lay on a table, as would a corpse, my hands bound on my chest, my feet also bound, and these retraints connected by a leather strop between them to minimize my movements. Above me, in the tiered watchtowers of the theater, an audience. They wore great masks of birds and jackals and unicorns, and other fantastical or otherworldly sorts. Other than this, they were naked,

The Necromancer

and the men's phalluses were at erection, the women's vaginas seemed enlarged—but it was only that they had been painted around the mons, reddened with face paint and rouge. As I noticed this fakery, I observed that the phallus of each man was not his own, but was also its own kind of mask—an exaggerated erection, designed by some perverse architect.

Standing before me, a man who wore a mask of a stag with great antlers, and his erection, too, was enormous, though I could see no outward sign that it was a counterfeit. His body was covered from chest to knees in an intricate mural of tattoos, images of creatures with mouths and tentacles, of orgies, and of faces too terrifying to describe here. It was an unspeakable canvas, and yet I could not help but look. As I watched the images, they seemed to move, and their lips opened, calling out, their arms wriggled along his skeletal muscularity. I noticed that his testicles and nipples, as well as navel, had the gemstones pressed into them, with a series of thin gold bands that hung from his member. It seemed both primitive, like islands found off the coast of a newly discovered world, with cannibals and headhunters, and yet, this was no doubt an Englishman, and, when I heard his voice, I knew who it was.

It was the owner of the Pandemonium.

¶

"You will die to the world," he said, his voice deep and calming. I felt at ease, despite my situation, as if something in his voice alone held power over me. "You will die as all men must die, but do not fear. You will this day find regeneration of body and soul, and you shall becomes one with us, the Golden Quivers of the Arrows of Apollo and of Baphomet and of Isis and of all who have been buried for thousands of years but who shall rise again through the chosen vessels."

Here, the others, watching me from above, cried out some litany in a language that I had never before heard.

"You shall learn the secrets of Magick, and the power of the Chymerical Realm, and gain dominion on this Earth, and speak with those who have spread themselves wide for the rape of Death," he said. Again, the litany rose from the crowd above us.

"You have been brought to us by a wandering spirit," he said. Here, he held his hands out, and a woman who wore a swan mask approached carrying a walnut box. She passed it to him, and then receded into the shadows. He opened the box, and held it aloft for the onlookers to see.

Then, he drew a small skull out of it, setting the box down at the edge of the stone table on which I lay.

"The will of the gods is strong!" he shouted, and the onlookers cheered. "I spent three years seeking out the secrets of the dead, and happened by a cemetery, consecrated by the unholy. A woman of great wealth, her spirit trapped by the very secrets she wished to keep, lay in her grave, unable to find release. I unburdened her, sacrificing a young child I had met along the way, letting the child's blood run into the grave so as to raise the woman from the dead that she might whisper of her treasures. But instead, another came to me, one who died as a baby, came to me and told me of his brother, this man you see before you, this one who has been known as Justin Gravesend to the world, but shall, after his first death, be known by a new name to us, born within the Chymera." Then, he brought the skull nearer my face. The stench was revolting, although perfumes had been applied to the skull, I could still scent disease and decay upon it. He pressed the skull to my lips, forcing me to kiss it, forcing the skull itself to kiss me, as well.

"Your brother told me of you. I knew that you were the one prophesied among the ancients and among our brethren, and the one of which many of the dead have spoken. Though you be a callow and pale youth who has ill-understood your role in the world, we have watched you, all of us!" He raised the small skull high, and the masked men and women cheered with renewed vigor. "You have been watched since that moment, followed, understood. We are out in the world, looking for such as you, looking for our Messiahs who have been foretold from the lips of the gods themselves. And you shall be the very incarnation of Baphomet! You shall be the one to open the doorway to the Veil, and bring the Age of Gods upon us!"

Somewhere, a thin reedy pipe began playing, and then a drum, its beat seeming ancient and strange. Not precisely musical or rhythmic, the watchers above us began a slow kind of dance that became a series of complicated, writhing embraces, and this cult of orgiasts began their revels.

The Master of Ceremonies, leaned over me, bringing the skull to my chest, and his lips to my ear. "Do not fear. Your brother had told me of the sign, and we have learned much of you. This has been ordained by the gods themselves."

He stood and set the skull in the wooden box.

Now, a young woman came into view, through the incense mist, wearing a thin gossamer tunic, as if she were an actress in a Greek tragedy. She wore no mask, nor veil did she have, and I recognized her immediately. With her own hands, she let slip her tunic, and stood before the infernal congregation, naked.

It was Anya, the beautiful young lady from my recent dinner, and the same that I dreamed I had seen between my schoolfriends in their whoring. The angel of purity who seemed to me now, a goddess from the netherworld itself. Her face was painted with occult symbols, and her breasts each sported the face of Baphomet. Her body scrawled across, in dark ink, words of another tongue. On her belly, above her delta, was the perfectly-rendered drawing of the Master himself who stood before her, his phallus erect and impossibly enormous, his teeth bared like a wolf's, his arms outstretched to clutch whomever pressed himself against this woman's body.

The Master of Ceremonies removed his mask, and as I knew, that alabaster face, and those beautiful gemstone eyes were behind it. He lifted Anya up and set her across my thighs. I struggled in my bonds, but found I had no movement. The more I struggled, the tighter my restraints became.

And there, on my body, the Master took her, with a hammering force that I felt in vibrations throughout my body, as if he were plunging himself into my own form. When he was done, he drew her up, holding her with one arm, he reached down to me with the other, to my wrists, to undo the restraints.

"This," he said. "Is the first sacrifice that shall save you from the embrace of Death herself."

The Necromancer

After my hands were free, and then my legs, he drew out that curious small blue flower and twirling vine from Anya's ringlets, and squeezed the petals into his hands. Then, he pressed his moistened fingers, with the pollen smell of the flower, against my lips, my nostrils, my eyes. Further, he rubbed the ointment—for that is what the crushed petals and vine became—into my privates, my fundament, and along the soles of my feet. Finally, with one thick droplet at the edge of his finger, he pressed this into my mouth, setting the warm burning bit of liquid on my tongue. It was sweet and bitter, reminding me of wormwood, and in consistency, viscous but smooth.

I felt its effects immediately, as if I had been hit, all at once, by a coach speeding by through a narrow alleyway. My body jerked as I felt the elixir's potency.

And then, the shadows and the congregation faded, and a whiteness, as of paint coming from an invisible artist's brush across the air, swept along the edges of my vision. I experienced a clarity, as if my breathing had become deeper, more calming to me. The whiteness, at first in thick brush strokes, then in a kind of mist, enveloped us, and all I could see was Anya, and the Master of Ceremonies himself.

"Many die when they part the Veil," the Master said. "The Lotos is poison to all but the chosen. You must now make the six sacrifices if you wish to reach your heart's desire, and your soul's longing."

As I was set free from all restraint, I felt something profound release from my mind, a great weight dropped, a mask being removed, like clouds moving out from a sun kept too long hidden from view.

As a dagger pressed into my hand, I had the first of my Visionaries, not merely visions, but a truly fundamental change in what I knew and experienced. I saw the woman before me, the woman I had known as Anya, the temple harlot, the unclean angel, the sacred whore, not as merely herself, but as the meat of the Gods.

I saw my flesh for what it was, the means of opening the sacrifice, of bringing the sacrifice into the realm of the divine.

The hole of flesh as a means of parting the Veil.

Surrounded by whiteness, I watched as small worms grew from my phallus, then from my arms, and from my mouth, a crawling mouth, a human mouth, a second set of teeth, yellowed and curved like the beak of a falcon, all snapping as the mouth emerged, lengthening. I was in communion with the gods. This was holy and not profane at all. These were the true commandments of the most holy: *that meat was the only food of the gods of power, and that I had truly been chosen, since the day of my birth, to perform this sacrifice of meat to the devourers that emerged from my own flesh.*

To rip open the hole.

To part the Veil.

To feed the gods.

Anya looked at me with her small mouth gasping like a fish which has been drawn by the fisherman from water. I went to encompass her, and I entered every part of her, my newborn tentacles finding the tiny pores of her skin and enlarging them as they burrowed beneath her flesh, my extended mouth ripping her lips, her gums, her tongue, her palate.

The Necromancer

10

So the day and night passed, and I learned of the sacred texts and read aloud from the *Grimoire Chymera* that had been passed from Hermes Trigestimus to the mortal Pandora to the Queen of Carthage, in whose library it was kept for centuries before the fires burned the magnificent Halls of Secrets of the Ancients. From there, it was taken into caves, into burial caverns, where from it, it is said the sacred Lotos grew, that flower of graveyards whose juice produces the poison Listanius, which kills a man on contact if he is not sanctified, or is the portal to the Veil for those who are chosen.

I spoke to the bones of my brother, and he told me of the secrets of Mother Death and the warmth of her bosom. The Master came to be known to me as the Necromancer, and he became more father to me than had my own father or my cherished uncle.

The Necromancer became my king.

But there was one knowledge I would only find, he told me, through my sacrifices. And so, I procured my friends James and Wendy, and others of theirs, the old admiral, a young man I found on the streets, the proprietress of the Pandemonium, Lady Caroline—and I opened each of them in turn and brought their meat to the gods.

11

And so, in my 21st year, I was reborn in the Chymera Magick. I had performed ritual murder, and taken all manner of hallucinogenic drug, including the Lotos that grew within the dankest of graves. I learned to raise the dead, and to speak with them, and learn of the treasures of the earth and of the air, and learned of their mysteries and their wisdoms. I ate of their flesh, and drank of their blood. I sacrificed, in my first year, many who offered themselves to me, calling me Messiah and Visionary.

But it was the Necromancer, the one who taught me these things, who brought me together with the others of the Chymerical Circle, to whom I owed my absolute allegiance.

It was he, my brother's bones in his hands, hearing the words of my brother, that brought him to seek me out, to send the Chymerians to find me in Manchester and to engineer my arrival in London, into a new life, through the Pandemonium. To raise the specters of old, to speak with Lucifage and Abaroeth and the Angel Azriel, and to understand the Veil and its denizens.

Of all these things, it is the power it has granted me that will remain with me forever, until the day I cross over into the Veil's milky shore.

And there, I will find him, my Necromancer, my Lord, my Master.

But until then, I will do as I have been asked.

I will find the treasures of the earth. I will raise great wealth. I will perform the sacrifices necessary.

And I will build the portal of the Veil one day, and keep it open unto the Earth and let the devourers of that realm enter this world and keep dominion over it.

Visionary Four

After the final of the six sacrifices, I squeeze two drops each in my eyes, just beneath the eyelid, and I close them once, to let the Veil enter my bloodstream by way of my vision.

I open my eyes again, their moist orbs burning with the acid of the Veil, and see the world turn to a foggy whiteness, and coming through its milky domain, a young man, of roughly my age, who looks very much like me.

I go to embrace my brother.

He whispers words that I can barely understand.

"What?" I ask.

He opens his mouth, which is filled with small worms and beetles crawling over his teeth, swarming up from his throat. They fly out from him, into the whiteness surrounding us, and they come toward me. I accept them, and through them I understand what he has wanted to let me know across the years between life and death.

The knowledge fills me with dread, for it was I myself who was destined to find the Devil and his henchman. I was marked even as a child.

My father had not murdered my brother, nor had my mother.

"Carry me to the water, look, and know the truth," the voice had told me as a child when I'd first dug up my brother's grave.

When I had looked into the water, I had seen my own reflection. That was what I had been meant to see. To know the truth.

It was I, even as a baby, who had turned in our blanket, using some implement unknown to me, some small sharp tool left by my father nearby, that I had used to break open my twin's skull, and steal his life. To leak his brains onto my shoulder even as I held him, struggling, in our birth-cradle.

My first human sacrifice to the gods of the Veil. They were there then, somehow, watching me. Watchers. Guiding my hand.

The mystery that has dogged my steps, is answered. The reason my father despised me and my mother prayed for my soul.

The mystery is no longer mystery. It is known to me. And understood.

I have seen the face of Baphomet, and it is the same face that I saw in the river when I was a boy. *Carry me to the water, look, and know the truth.*

I am Cain, himself. I am the very Beast.

I am the Monster. I am now the Necromancer himself.

A ystyrio, cofied
Let him who reflects, remember.

Afterword

I wanted to include a brief note here about the mythos I am creating between various works. Mythos-building in horror is something I don't see much of in the 21st century, although some writers do it and do it phenomenally well (King's *Dark Tower* mythos, for example.)

When I began writing my novel, *Nightmare House*, I had no real sense that building up of a backstory about the supernatural creation of a haunted house would spawn a few other novels, including *Mischief*, *The Infinite*, and now, *The Necromancer*.

In doing so, I began to search my own beliefs within the "fantastic" realm of darkness and horror, and I wanted to remake the mythology of the world as if I were somehow writing the history of another humankind on another earth. Truthfully, I want the creatures of night to exist. I want to be able to touch the gods. I want a world where those things are not mythological, but could happen.

But in building that world—the story of the people who are somehow associated with a house called Harrow that spans more than 100 years -- I also began to build a mythos backward to a saga, most of which I had written and hidden away, many years back. It's called *The Vampyricon,* and its first book, coming up in 2004 is *The Priest of Blood.* Even it is an underground book in many ways.

Unlike my other novels, *The Priest of Blood* is an epic dark fantasy of vampirism and sorcery, eroticism and death cults, set in a medieval world, but reaching back in scope to a more ancient time. It is in *The Vampyricon* that I explore the underpinnings of such things that grow in the centuries as the Chymera Magick, the Veil, and even an idea I have not fully finished with, which is the Dark Madonna, Mother Death mentioned in *The Necromancer.*

The covers of the lettered and limited edition hardcovers of *The Necromancer* have images created specifically for *The Vampyricon.* But because the character of the Necromancer is a direct descendant of "The Fallen One" and "The Pythoness," both Rich Chizmar, the publisher of Cemetery Dance, Caniglia, the artist, and I felt that these captured the spirit of the world of the Necromancer, even though the two stories are set many centuries apart.

For those who read my novels consistently, I appreciate your staying with them, and piecing together the excavation of this supernatural underworld of men, gods, and monsters that cross between the Harrow mythos and the Vampyricon.

Douglas Clegg
April 24, 2003